The Last Man off the Mountain

By
Daris Howard

Publishing Inspiration

The Last Man off the Mountain
By
Daris W. Howard

Copyright © 2022
by
Daris W. Howard

ISBN-10: 1-62986-029-8
ISBN-13: 978-1-62986-029-9

www.publishinginspiration.com

Publishing Date: January 9, 2023

Publishing Inspiration LLC

Table of Contents

I dedicate this book to my oldest son, Scott, and his family. I often took my two young boys on overnight camping with the scouts when we weren't doing anything intense.
Daris Howard

I also pay honor and tribute to the extraordinary men and women I have had the privilege of knowing in my life in scouting. I especially recognize the incredible scouts I had in my troop, and also my assistants and others who worked with me.
Daris Howard

1
The Important Assignment

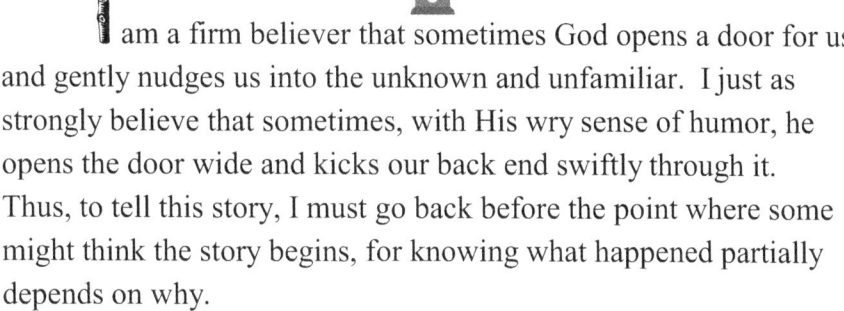

I am a firm believer that sometimes God opens a door for us and gently nudges us into the unknown and unfamiliar. I just as strongly believe that sometimes, with His wry sense of humor, he opens the door wide and kicks our back end swiftly through it. Thus, to tell this story, I must go back before the point where some might think the story begins, for knowing what happened partially depends on why.

I can't say that I was one to aspire to be a scoutmaster. I, myself, am an Eagle Scout and enjoyed the scouting program. However, that was in my younger years, back when my body didn't wince at sleeping on the ground, tramping miles upon miles through the mountains, and freezing within an inch of death. Those were great days, and I enjoyed them, but I had long since given them up for the creature comforts of life: a warm, soft bed and a porcelain seat to sit on when nature called. But I am getting ahead of myself, for the premise is set, but the reason is not yet told.

In the lay congregation where we attended church in our rural community, I had become an assistant to the man who was the congregational leader whom we called "Bishop" or "the bishop." Though some might say this was a prestigious assignment, it also carried great responsibility. The three of us who oversaw the congregation rotated months being responsible for Sunday's main church meeting. We needed to make sure we had a proper speaker, music, and any other religious occurrence appropriate for the meeting.

In addition, we needed to make sure all other needs of the congregation and community were filled. This included both Sunday assignments, such as Sunday School Teachers, and non-Sunday assignments, such as scout leaders.

There must have been something in the water for a few years, for almost everyone having a child had a boy. There were eighteen boys, to be exact, in the six-to-twelve-year age group, most of whom were six to eight years old. There were only two girls of that same age. The large number of boys made finding cub scout leaders challenging. That many boys wore out a cub scout leader almost monthly. And when the last of the boys was approaching the even more strenuous years of scouting, keeping the scoutmaster position filled was nearly impossible. Some men we asked to take on the assignment moved from the community. I don't know if that directly resulted from our request, but our options for leaders lessened dramatically.

As the last of the boys turned twelve, we deliberated many hours about who would be best to put into the assignment of scoutmaster. He had to be firm, patient, and have a strong scout background.

The man we finally settled on was Harry Ward. It was true that he was an avid scouter, a patient man, and yet firm. He had been an eagle scout, raised a large family, and was a vigorous supporter on our scout committee. His hard work in the scouting program had earned him the honor of Silver Beaver, one of scouting's highest honors. But the main reason we chose him was because he came to us and requested the job.

Out of the three of us, I was the only one who expressed reservations about Harry's lack of time with the boys in the field. I had gone many times as a volunteer. I had hiked, camped, eaten burnt food, laid in a sleeping bag, unable to sleep, and followed nature's call behind many a bush. I knew that working on support committees and taking on the assignment of scoutmaster were far different. Usually, scoutmasters came up through the rough trenches, starting first as assistant scoutmaster to learn the ropes.

But we were in a desperate situation, as the current scoutmaster was moving, thus triggering our search. Word was those few that had already been scoutmasters and knew we were looking got caller ID and screened their calls in case we tried to put them into the assignment again. And the current scoutmaster's reason for leaving the community was a little sketchy, leading us to wonder if dealing with the eighteen boys had driven him to insanity. No one else that would reasonably accept the assignment had nearly as many qualifications as Harry. Besides, the final clincher was that Harry was a second-grade teacher and had summers free for camping.

Though I was the one that was most concerned because I was also the one that had spent the most time camping with the boys, I finally had to admit that we were out of options. We talked to Harry and told him we had decided the assignment should be his.

He was excited. "After all these years, I finally get to be the scoutmaster. I have always wanted to be one. I was an assistant years ago, but I've never been the scoutmaster."

Hearing he had been an assistant set my mind at ease considerably—at first. I learned it was with a city troop, and I soon realized that those boys were far different.

Harry was excited and ready to jump right in. Thus, with the confirmation of the committee and others involved, the next Tuesday night, the night the troop met at the church, Harry was there to take charge.

When we asked him if he had anyone in mind as an assistant, he just laughed. "Why would I need an assistant? I know pretty much everything there is to know about scouting. When we go camping, I will just get some dads to go along."

And then he added something else. "And the first thing I'm going to get rid of is playing that silly basketball at scout meetings."

"But Harry," I said, "these boys work hard, and they look forward to some fun playing basketball. Maybe a little compromise of some work and then some play would be good."

"It teaches them the wrong thing," Harry replied. "It makes them think that scouting is all play and not about learning. You give them an inch, and they'll take a mile."

All these statements struck fear into my heart. I, too, had done a lot of training, but I was the opposite. The more I learned, the less I felt I knew about running a scout troop. But Harry's confidence, in turn, increased that of everyone else on our committee.

Now, I will not sugarcoat reality and say we had perfect boys. The young men in our troop were typical farm boys. They worked hard and, when they had time off, they wanted to play hard. Most changed pipe early in the morning and late in the evening, and during the day they worked hard on other farm labor. Scout meetings were not a formal affair, and wearing a uniform was something they only planned to do at a court of honor, if then.

Harry had been to hundreds of scout training sessions, but nothing could prepare him for the resistance he met in the boys the first night as he tried to cajole, bribe, joke, and threaten them into wearing their uniforms. I stayed for a short time, but I had to leave for a meeting.

Fortunately, we had our congregational leadership meeting the same night. I say fortunately because, when we took a break, and I stepped into the church gym, I found the whole group of boys playing ball, and Harry was not there. When I asked the boys where he was, they nonchalantly said he was still in the scout room. I was surprised that he let the scout  meeting out so early. I wandered down to the scout room. As I neared it, I could hear a muffled cry for help. I quickened my pace, trotting, then running. I found Harry tied up in the scout closet.

As I untied him, I asked, "Harry, what happened?"

Harry was mad. "After they refused to even consider wearing their uniforms, I tried to teach them their knots."

I tried not to smile. To our rough-and-tumble farm boys, ropes only meant one thing—something to tie something up with, or more drastically, something to tie some**one** up with.

"I started explaining some of the standard knots," Harry fumed. "They said they knew how to tie knots and 'didn't need no stupid lesson on it.' So, I told them to show me. Oh, sure, they tied knots, some of the ugliest knots I have ever seen. None of them seemed to know what a standard knot was. I told them, 'Those knots would come undone at the first tug.'"

That was his first mistake.

I swallowed hard to not smile as he said, "They dared me to show them that I could get untied. I decided to take their challenge."

That was his second mistake.

A farm boy may not know how to tie a scout handbook type of knot, but he knows how to tie a knot that will not come undone. Thus, Harry found himself pretty much hogtied as the boys wrapped him with rope and pulled the knots tight. Having a little too much pride to beg to be untied, he worked his way into the scout closet to find a nail or something he could hook a piece of the knot on to undo the rope.

That was his third mistake. The boys shut the door, put a chair under the doorknob so he couldn't get out, and they were off to play basketball. It makes a person wonder what would have happened if I hadn't wandered down to the scout room.

As Harry told the story, his anger increased. When he finished, he headed down to round the boys up and bring them back to the scout room and shut down that ". . . ridiculous basketball playing once and for all so they could get to important scouting training."

"Harry," I said, "perhaps it would be a good idea to join the boys in a basketball game. Get to know them and be their friend."

He glared at me. "These boys don't need a friend. They need someone they can look up to. You don't become such a person by being their friend. You've got to be on higher ground to lift them."

I had to admit that sounded good in theory, but there had to be a balance between being the leader figure and being their friend. Harry would have none of it. Being tied up in the closet had frosted his attitude, and I was glad he didn't have a bullwhip. He soon had the reluctant boys rounded up and back in the scout room.

I made my way back to the second part of my meeting. When it ended, I was surprised to see the boys playing basketball again. Actually, I wasn't, but I thought that Harry, after being tied up, had surely learned his lesson. I was also sure he wasn't about to let them play any basketball that night. Then I considered that I ought to check the scout room again.

As I headed in that direction, I told myself there was surely no way that Harry could be locked up again. He was too smart to fall for something like that twice. I leisurely wandered down there until I heard the muffled calls for help and quickened my pace.

I found Harry once again locked in the scout closet, madder than a bull in a red pen. He was throwing his entire weight against the door, but he was skinny, and the chair under the doorknob continued to hold. I opened the closet door to find Harry so fired up he could have boiled water on his balding head. "Did you know that stupid doorknob is just the right height for a chair to block it shut? I am either going to remove the knob completely or move it higher so they can't ever put a chair under it and lock me in here again," he hollered.

I had to admit I did know that a chair could block the door shut. The scouts often locked each other in there that way. I had been meaning to move the doorknob higher myself. I just never got around to it.

"What happened this time?" I asked.

As he spoke, his voice thundered with frustration. "The scout handbook suggests we play a game to end the scout meeting, so I brought 'pin the tail on the donkey' to finish up the evening."

6

I could imagine how well that went across with twelve to seventeen-year-old boys. I once again carefully held back my grin to alleviate inflaming the already agitated scoutmaster as he continued. "The boys suggested I go first, and after I was blindfolded, they spun me around and spun me right into the closet, shut the door, and propped the chair under the doorknob."

I swallowed twice to get the laugh out of my voice and then spoke. "Maybe you could work out a compromise with the boys and let them play basketball at the end of scout meetings for the game at the end."

"Over my dead body," Harry growled. "That is a useless game that teaches you nothing!"

I was about to ask what "pin the tail on the donkey" taught a person, especially when one is locked in a closet, but I thought better of it. As an infuriated Harry headed for the gym, the parents started arriving to pick up their sons. They were just in time, I thought, to save the boys' lives. Those whose parents were late picking them up caught one look at Harry's purplish-red face, and they were quick to catch rides with the other boys.

I thought this might dampen Harry's exuberance as a scout leader, but Harry wasn't anything if he wasn't persistent. A day hadn't passed before he put a new doorknob higher on the scout closet, one he made sure could not be locked from the outside. He moved all the religious pictures to one wall so he could load a wall with scouting pictures on Tuesday nights. It made the room look lopsided on Sundays when the scout pictures were stored away in the closet. But when the Sunday school teacher who taught in there wanted to put her pictures back, she quickly backed down when she realized Harry had already been pushed too far.

The problem was, the boys had only begun to push. Harry was sure all he needed to "get the boys with him" was a good campout. After the exciting scout night, I thought it might be good for them to plan it for a time when I could join them to help, but Harry assured me he had it all under control. He had a couple of dads coming along.

It was late fall, and the weather was always unpredictable. It could change from sunny to raining and snowing with no sign it was coming. When the boys loaded up late on a Friday afternoon, there was not a cloud in the sky. But by the time they had hit the mountains a couple of hours away, a deluge was coming out of the sky that would have made Noah quiver. I couldn't help but wonder how the scouts were doing as I lay in my nice, warm bed that night.

On Saturday, I had meetings all day, so I could not check on them. On Sunday, I didn't even have to ask how it all went as I looked at Harry. His already receding hairline was far more receded, and his eyebrows were nonexistent. He still smelled of soot and singed hair, even though I'm sure he had tried to shower it away. I casually asked him how it went.

He spoke in broken sentences, seemingly only half coherent. "Couldn't get a fire started. One dad had a can of gas in his truck. Thought we'd try it. Didn't think it could hurt. Just a little gas. Didn't mean to catch the whole can on fire! Burned down the scout tent and all the supplies. Fought the fire half the night. Didn't think a fire could burn like that in a rainstorm. Almost lost both pickups and the van."

He shook his head and continued to babble on. It would have been funny if it hadn't been so sad. I wondered if he would ever recover, but by Tuesday night, he was back to his confident self. We bought them a new scout tent, and we suggested that he probably could use an assistant, but he was not ready to back down yet. Scout month was barely two months away, and he was looking forward to shaping the boys up for the Klondike Derby. He could envision dozens of merit badges hanging on the board at the scout banquet.

The meeting nights seemed to be a tug-of-war from then on between Harry and the boys. He did learn that the boys were not interested in pin-the-tail-on-the-donkey. He tried some other scout games with more success, but it never seemed to make up for the fact they wanted to play basketball. The number of boys coming to the meetings was dwindling, and we started to worry about the young men in our community.

As the Klondike Derby approached, there seemed to be heightened interest among the boys. Their attendance picked back up as they made plans for this annual winter campout.

The Klondike Derby is a significant event in our small community. The scout troops from all over the district meet and camp overnight. Then, the following day, they test their preparedness skills against each other. Harry had them practicing compass courses around the outside of the church, ice rescue across the parking lot, and fire building in the park fire pit. There seemed to be a bit of exuberance returning to the troop, though the underlying tension of not getting to release their pent-up energy playing basketball at the end of the night still lingered.

Finally, the weekend of the Klondike Derby arrived. I had hoped to go with them but ended up having another assignment. It was okay, Harry assured me. He had plenty of dads going with him. I was leery. Many of the dads I knew thought winter camping was comprised of a rented cabin for a weekend. But there was nothing I could do about it. I was there when they packed up and prepared their gear at the scout meeting before the derby, and all seemed in order.

Friday night came and went, and my apprehension was fading. But then early Saturday morning, I mean really early, like two o'clock, the phone began ringing and never seemed to stop. It started with irate parents concerned about the welfare of their sons, and the last call was from a worried scoutmaster's wife. Harry was in the hospital awaiting hernia surgery. The boys were alive and would soon be no worse for wear, though some were suffering from severe hypothermia and light burns. The fathers who had been on the campout were ready to take up arms against us, their leaders. The situation was bad, and to make matters worse, I couldn't even find out what had happened. I had found out that the directors of the Klondike Derby had asked our troop to go home, but that's as far as I got.

I canceled my other assignments that Saturday and went to visit Harry. He was sleeping, and the doctor said he'd be all right. Nothing a good surgery and six weeks of recovery couldn't heal. When I saw Harry, all his hair burned away, slight burn blisters on his arms and face, and his eyebrows that had just barely started recovering were totally gone, I knew things weren't good. I asked Harry what had happened. He only said he didn't want to talk about it.

Meeting with the boys, the dads, and the other scout leaders in the community, I finally pieced it all together. As soon as they arrived at the campsite, Harry, seeing a groomed snowmobile trail, decided that was the right road. He drove onto it, followed by the other dads, and soon all three vehicles were stuck tight. They dug and shoveled and pushed until one o'clock in the morning to get them out, all the while having no food and no camp set up. By the time they got the vehicles out, they were cold and sweaty, but even though Harry had already gotten a hernia, he was still dogged determined to make this a success.

The boys and the dads laid straw on the snow and set the tent on it while Harry tried to start a fire. The breeze kept blowing the matches out, so he decided to build the fire in the tent and then move it out to the fire pit. The fire caught the straw on fire, the straw caught the tent on fire, the tent caught the supplies on fire, the supplies caught the kerosene cookstove on fire, and the ensuing explosion caught the next camp on fire. From there, there was a chain reaction from campsite to campsite and troop to troop. By the time the fire department came, almost every troop had lost gear, and some barely escaped with their lives. The Search and Rescue group that directed the Klondike competition had lost a snow machine.

They would have lost more if they hadn't braved the inferno to get the pickups and Suburbans away. When I talked to the Search and Rescue director to offer my apologies, he said, "The only good that came from it was that we were able to show the boys what **NOT** to do."

An emergency meeting of the scout committee and the parents was called for Sunday. One father expressed the opinion of the other parents. "I'm not against Harry and all. He's a good man. It's just that we feel our boys would be a whole lot safer if you can keep Harry away from them."

In addition, a couple of days later, we received a certified letter from the scout office saying that if we didn't change our troop leadership, they would revoke our charter.

The decision was made, with Harry's agreement, that we needed to find another scoutmaster. But who could it be? Very few would take on the challenge of eighteen boys, especially these eighteen boys. We had pretty much exhausted our list of candidates. The Bishop said he wanted to take some time to pray and ponder the issue.

As the day progressed, I started getting strange feelings about being scoutmaster. Maybe it was just because I was the one with the most experience in the field with the boys. But I think it is interesting how that works in life. I wonder if it's God's way of preparing you so when he opens the door and kicks your hide through it, you don't expire on the spot from surprise. Whatever it was, by the time I received the phone call late one night, I knew what was coming. The bishop said he wanted to meet with me in his office at the church. He was already there and said he was waiting for me.

After I arrived at the church, he invited me into his office and asked me to take a seat.

"Tom," he said, "I'm afraid what I want to talk to you about will offend you. I know the position you now have is considered somewhat of a prestigious job in our community, and any release from it could be viewed as a demotion, even causing people to think the person might have done something wrong. But what I have to say is very important. I just don't know quite how to say it."

At this point, I interjected, "Bishop, if you want to release me from my assignment and put me in as scoutmaster, that's fine."

He looked at me with astonishment. "You knew?"

"I've had a feeling all afternoon that is what should happen. And I'm not sure who else could work with these boys."

He smiled a relieved smile. "And you don't have a problem with that?"

I shook my head. "I must admit, I have doubts about my ability to deal with some of the challenges of being a scoutmaster. But if I can help these boys grow to be good, honorable men, there could be nothing of greater value I could do. And if I am doing what God wants, it doesn't really matter what my assignment is. If he wanted me to be the person to hold the door at church, then I would hope that I would say yes and work to be the best door holder He had ever had."

The bishop smiled and got up to shake my hand. "I think you will be the best scoutmaster, too."

As I left his office, the doubts about the last statement filled my mind with a storm of concern. Eighteen boys is a lot of boys, especially these boys. They were at a critical point in their lives. I could remember my own teenage years and the good leaders I had. I could also think of a few that left us on our own to make our way the best we could. I hoped I could be the kind of leader these boys needed and do for them what my good leaders did for me.

*****

It took the rest of the week to get the stamp of approval from the scout committee and the parents, but by the following Sunday, I was officially the scoutmaster for our troop.

As I walked out of church that Sunday, I took a deep breath. I knew I was taking on a big assignment, but little did I know the impact it would have on me and how much it would change my life.

2

A Matter of Compromise

There were many things I needed to do to start things rolling the way I wanted. The first was to get myself a capable assistant. One thing I was sure of was that I couldn't take on this assignment alone. I chose a man who, though not a churchgoer, was a man of the outdoors. I knew he was a good man, even if he was a rugged individual. He had a rough beard and long hair. He looked like a mountain man, and his demeanor matched his looks.

I received permission from the congregational leadership and the scout committee to approach him about the assignment. I drove to his house to visit with him. He was very congenial, and I was surprised that he had already learned of my change in assignment. He laughed as he invited me in. "I suppose it's safe enough. After all, I know you aren't here to drag me to church or to ask me to talk in a meeting or something."

I smiled and appreciated his friendliness. We chatted for a minute, and then I got right to the point. "Rod," I said, "I don't know if you know why I'm here."

"Well," he replied, "I have my ideas. But why don't you tell me for sure, and then we'll both know."

"As you might know," I said, "there are a lot of boys in our community that are of scouting age. There is no way that I can deal with them alone. I need help and would like you to be the assistant scoutmaster."

He stroked his chin thoughtfully for a short time. "You wouldn't expect me to attend church every week, would you?"

"I would love to have your help on Sunday," I replied, "but if not, I'll settle for your help on Tuesdays for scout meetings when I especially need it."

In our church, the person who worked as scoutmaster usually also taught the lessons to the same boys in their class on Sunday. We felt the consistency between the scouting during the week, and the religious training on Sunday strengthened the young men.

I told Rod we had another man that would join me with the boys on Sunday, so it would be optional even though we would like to have him there.

"How many boys are there?" he queried further.

"There are fourteen boys currently participating in the troop, and another four I hope to visit to see if I can get them to join."

He gulped slightly. "Eighteen boys? Do you know what you've gotten yourself into?"

I nodded. "That's why I came to you for help. I have some ways of keeping order, and I'm good in the outdoors, but you're better. I need the best person I can get."

He eyed me suspiciously as if he wasn't sure I was paying him a compliment just to get him to say yes. In all honesty, there was no other man I felt I would prefer with me in a challenging situation in the wilds. He thought deeply about the assignment and seemed to waver. His wonderful wife joined us, bringing in a plate of cookies. At her questioning, I filled her in on my purpose for being there. When I finished, Rod turned to her. "Hon, what do you think?"

"Oh, Rod," she replied. "This would be a great opportunity for you, and I know you would do a fantastic job."

"What boys are in the troop?" Rod asked.

I handed him the list of boys, sorted from oldest to youngest.

David Handon
Morton (Mort) Talbot
Gordan (Gordy) Hider
Steven Deidrick
Dexter Henderson
Devin Oberle
Dallin Oberle

Justin Rider
Tanner Halstrom
Alex Handon
Sam Fredricks
Mike Sylvester
Mark Sylvester
Seth Hensley
Jason Hamilton
Jared Davidson
Jeremy Hilliard
Chester Neely

Rod looked at it for a moment and let out a long breath. "Eighteen boys, including both the Oberle and Sylvester twins. And Mort and Gordy, who can't seem to ever stay out of trouble. This is quite the group."

"That's why I don't want to attempt this alone."

"Seriously," Rod said, "every one of them reminds me of myself when I was their age, and I wouldn't want to have been my scoutmaster, let alone try to help direct eighteen boys like me."

I laughed. "I've had some similar thoughts. But I considered that might be the whole reason for me to be in there. I have an idea of the shenanigans these boys might pull."

Rod laughed. "Shenanigans. You're dating yourself using a fifty-dollar word like that."

I knew Rod's wife wanted him to do more in the church, and she seemed to think this might be a start. She gently touched his arm. "This is right up your alley, Rod. Besides, you might enjoy taking our sons with you."

He looked at his boys, romping on the floor. They were seven and nine years old. "I plan to take my own boys when I can," I added.

He nodded, slowly at first, as if in thought, then more and more. Finally, he looked me straight in the eye. "Why not? It might be interesting. But there is one other thing I don't do."

"What's that?" I asked.

"I am not a scouter, never have been, and don't plan to be. I will teach them what I know of the outdoors and camping, but that merit badge stuff is up to you."

I nodded and smiled. "Agreed."

We spent another hour or more talking about the troop and the logistics of what lay ahead. What he had thought I was coming for was a donation to resupply the troop equipment list. He had heard about the disaster at the Klondike Derby and figured I was trying to restock everything. He had been shocked at the true nature of my visit, but he did have equipment and supplies he said he would be willing to donate. I had some as well. We listed everything else we needed, and I took the list to the scout committee. They promised to canvas the community for donations.

The next job was to meet with the boys. Tuesday came too soon. Even though the parents had not yet approved Rod, the scout committee had given us the green light, so he joined me Tuesday night. We pulled all the boys reluctantly from the basketball court into the scout room.

As I looked out at the fourteen boys that were there, a feeling of inadequacy came over me, but there was no looking back.

"I'm glad you all came tonight for our scout meeting," I said. Some of them looked defiant, others bored, and some just stared at the floor, so I couldn't tell what they were thinking. I forged on. "First off, I want to know what you young men want from the scouting program."

Gordy, shouted, "We just want to play basketball!" With that, he jumped up and headed for the door.

Rod stepped in front of the door and folded his arms. "And just where do you think you're going?"

"Uh, I was going to play basketball," Gordy said timidly. "I thought we were done."

"We're done when we say we're done," Rod growled.

Gordy slipped back into his seat. I nodded my thanks to Rod as I continued. "I like to play basketball as much as anybody, but I know your parents send you over here to gain the values and training that scouting offers. Still, I think there's room for both."

"We can split the time. If we work hard for 45 minutes on scouting, we can have the last 45 minutes for basketball."

They nodded, but I wanted a firm commitment, so I asked anyone who could not support that plan to stand. Gordy and Mort started to stand, then Gordy caught a glare from Rod and sank back into his seat. Mort followed.

I told them that would mean we had to be ready to start on time. If we couldn't get them into the scout room and get started as we should, that time would have to come off their basketball time. They grumbled briefly, but again everyone agreed.

Next, we laid out our agenda and what they wanted to do. We discussed the different merit badges. They wanted to get camping, fishing, and mountain climbing. The last, due to my fear of heights, made me shiver, but I wrote it on the chalkboard. I told them we expected service, which was part of scouting. They rolled their eyes but agreed to do service one week per month. The forty-five minutes were quickly coming to a close, and there was one more thing I wanted to discuss.

"What about wearing uniforms?" I asked. Instantly, there was a groan.

"Don't tell us you plan to make us dress up like sissies!" Gordy said.

"Yeah," Devin joined in, "uniforms are stupid."

There seemed to be general agreement on that issue. If there is one thing I learned from watching Harry with the troop, it is that there are certain battles that aren't worth fighting.

"All right," I said, "what if we compromise? You don't have to wear your uniform anywhere except for court of honors, scout advancements, and being part of a color guard or other such ceremonies when we are showing respect to our flag and country."

"Does that include scout camp?" Mort asked.

"We'll consider scout camp as a separate issue and discuss it later." It was getting to the end of our forty-five minutes, and I wanted the young men to know I would keep my word.

They, too, wanted to get out and play basketball, so they agreed. I told them I would write up what we had discussed and have it for each of them to sign the following week. With that, the scout meeting adjourned to the basketball court.

The boys were surprised when I joined them. I was surprised when Rod did as well. He was not only good at basketball, but he was good while wearing big work boots. The older boys told us we were two old men and said they could whip us. We took their challenge. We took the six smallest boys onto our team, and they took the eight biggest boys on theirs.

It wasn't even close. In my years in New York, I had learned to play tough street ball, and if I was anywhere near the basket, the rebounds were mine, even up against Gordy, who was an inch taller than me. A quick pass to Rod, and as he thundered down the court in his big work boots, the boys seemed to scatter in front of him. We tried to pass it to the boys on our team, but when they saw one of the bigger boys bearing down on them, they were quick to jettison it right back to us.

By the time the first parents arrived to pick up their boys, I was covered with sweat, and my heart was pounding. But as Gordy turned to leave, he high-fived me. "You're all right for an old man," he said. And then he did the same to Rod.

In that instant, I knew we truly were accepted as scoutmasters, and we had our troop.

3
The Last Man Off the Mountain

The next couple of weeks found me trying in every way possible to contact the other four boys in our troop. My assignment included all boys in our rural community, whether or not they were part of our church. I knew two of the four boys that did not attend the scout meetings quite well, but two of the boys named on my roster I had never met. The first two attended church, but they never came to scouts. The second two didn't even attend church.

I turned to the boys that already came to scouts to learn about the other four. I knew they would understand the other young men their age better than I would. At the next scout meeting, I broached the subject of why their friends didn't attend.

"What about Jason Hamilton?" I asked.

"Good luck getting him to come," Gordy said. "He doesn't like camping."

"But we do more than camping," I said. "Maybe he would at least like to come for those things."

"Can't hurt to try," Gordy said.

"How about Sam Fredricks?" I asked.

"I think Sam would like to come," Gordy said. "But his mother is afraid of everything. She will hardly let him out of the house for fear something awful will happen to him."

"Maybe I can go talk to her," I replied.

"I think he would be really grateful," Devon replied.

"The last two I show on the list are brothers," I said. "Their names are Alex and David Handon. I know David, but does anyone know Alex?"

The boys looked back and forth at each other but didn't say anything. It was Mort who finally answered. "None of us like to go over there. Their dad is often drunk, and he isn't very nice."

"But I hear he is quite outdoorsy," I replied. The boys didn't say anything, but just looked back and forth among themselves.

"Can't hurt to try," Gordy said.

"But be careful going there," Mort added.

"Why?" I asked.

The boys all looked at each other, then Gordy said, "Because their dad can be mean when he's drunk, which is most of the time."

I decided to start with Jason. I went to his house and knocked on the door. His dad answered. This was the first time I had met him, so I introduced myself and explained the purpose of my visit.

The father was a small man with big glasses and ruffled brown hair. I knew he was an accountant or something like that. He had the total look of a nerd. Jason's mother was a bit bigger than her husband, but she, too, looked like she would be less than comfortable in an environment of physical outdoor activities.

They invited me to sit down and offered me a comfortable chair. They positioned themselves on the couch across from me.

Mr. Hamilton turned to his wife. "Mr. Johnson is here to talk to us and Jason about Jason joining the scout troop."

"I think that would be good for him," Mrs. Hamilton said.

"I do, too," Mr. Hamilton said. "But I'm not sure how Jason would feel about it."

He then turned and called for Jason. A moment later, a boy, smaller than any other boy in the troop, appeared in the doorway. "Yes, Dad?" he said.

"Mr. Johnson is here to see if you would like to join the scout troop," Mr. Hamilton said.

Jason shrugged. "I'm not really into camping. It's so dirty, and there are so many bugs."

"We don't just go camping," I replied. "We learn to tie knots. We go hiking and all sorts of things."

I could tell by the look on his face that I was not helping him want to join us. I thought a minute, and then I said, "And there are also lots of merit badges that we work on."

"Like what?" he asked.

I looked at him and considered a few things before I finally answered. "There are things like music, engineering, and computers. Besides, you can earn an Eagle Scout, which is good to have on a resume."

That seemed to really help. "Could I learn those things without camping?"

"You would need some camping to get an Eagle, but you could definitely work on merit badges without going camping. And if there are any of those things that you have expertise on, you can share it with the others."

Mrs. Hamilton said, "Jason, why don't you try it for a while and see what you think?"

Jason slowly, reluctantly, nodded. His parents filled out the paperwork for him and said he would be there the following week.

I went from there to Sam Fredrick's house. I knew his mother. Everyone called her Marissa, but I didn't know what she used for her last name. She was divorced from an abusive husband, and I thought she might have taken back her maiden name.

When I told her what I was there for, Marissa looked at her son as she answered. "I don't know. I hear that scouting is kind of dangerous."

"But, Mom," Sam said, "I've always wanted to . . ."

Marissa cut him off. "Lots of people want to do crazy things. That doesn't mean they should."

"Besides teaching the boys things like survival skills," I said, "we have a lot of fun and play basketball and things. It will give him a good chance to associate with other boys his age doing wholesome activities."

She paused a moment, looked at her son's pleading face, and then turned to me. "But I hear you go camping and do dangerous activities?"

I shrugged. "I don't know that I would call them dangerous. But it is true that we go camping, hiking, and things like that. The scouting program feels it is important for a boy to learn survival skills and be able to take care of themselves if they get lost somewhere or something."

"Please, Mom!" Sam said.

"We also learn skills for merit badges in all sorts of fields, like engineering, music, and computers," I said.

Marissa looked one more time at her son's face. She slowly nodded. I handed her the paper to fill out. As she was filling it out, she said, "Well, at least I don't have to worry about you camping for half of the year. It's too cold to camp in the winter."

She looked up at me and smiled, and I didn't say anything, but the look on my face must have. She stopped filling out the paper. "You don't go camping in the winter, do you?"

"Well, uh . . ."

"You do, don't you?" she said. "Are you crazy, going out in the freezing cold here in the winter in Idaho? I could see it in California or something, but not here! I don't plan to send my son out with some crazy scoutmaster!" She ripped up the form and tossed it at me.

"Marissa," I said, "winter is half the year around here."

"Don't you think I know that?" she replied haughtily. "In fact, I'd say the stupid cold is far more than half."

"What will you do if your son is caught out in the cold somewhere?"

"What makes you think he will be?"

"Because it happens all the time. A young person could be coming home from school and have their car break down or anything like that. Our job is to train the boys so they have the skills they need to survive in whatever environment they're caught in. We take good care of them and make sure they're safe. I feel for us to not teach them how to survive in winter could be detrimental to them."

Marissa breathed deeply, trying to calm herself. She seemed to be thinking about what I said. She looked at her son again, and his face showed how much he wanted to be a scout. She turned back to me. "Do you promise he will be safe?"

"I promise you the boys will be safe," I replied. "Rod and I are well-trained in outdoor skills, and we love these boys. I would give my life to protect each and every one of them."

Suddenly, tears came to Marissa's eyes, and she could not hold them back. "I wish he had a father that felt that way." She was quiet for a moment, and when she spoke, her voice was quiet. "I will sign the paper," she said. "But not because I am excited about him camping and doing dangerous things, but because I feel he needs the example of good men." But then she spoke strongly as she added, "But if I feel things are too dangerous, I will pull him out."

I nodded. "That's only fair."

I gave her a second paper, and she started filling it out again. When she finished, I reached out and shook Sam's hand as I stepped to the door. He grinned uncontrollably. When I reached out to shake Marissa's hand, she held my hand and looked me in the eye. "He will be safe?"

I nodded. "I'll protect and teach him as I would my own son."

She nodded and dropped my hand.

The last house was that of Alex and David. Alex was only fourteen years old, but his brother, David, was seventeen. I knew David because he had done things off and on with the troop and even came to church now and then. But I didn't know Alex at all. I also knew Mrs. Handon because she came to church with David. She was a nice lady. But Mr. Handon never came to church, and I had only a brief acquaintance with him in the community.

It was with a fair amount of trepidation that I knocked on their door. David was the one who opened it. He smiled. "Mr. Johnson. It's good to see you. Come in."

As I stepped in, I shook his hand. "Hi, David. I guess you have heard that I am the new scoutmaster?"

He nodded. "I've been thinking about coming back to scouts. I am a Life Scout and need to finish my Eagle."

"That would be great," I replied. "I was hoping Alex might want to come, too."

David didn't say anything for a moment, and the silence was slightly awkward. When he did speak, he only said, "Maybe you should talk to my parents."

David led me into the living room. Mr. Handon was sitting on a couch with the television blaring in front of him. He was unshaven and had no shirt on. The coffee table right in front of him was littered with beer cans. When he saw me, he frowned.

I reached out my hand to him. "Hi, Mr. Handon, I'm Tom Johnson."

He didn't even pretend to be friendly and did not shake my hand. "I know who you are."

"I'm the new scoutmaster," I said.

"I know," he replied. "I heard much of your scout supplies were destroyed. Did you come to beg for money for your stupid troop? If you did, you can just go back where you came from."

"Actually, I didn't. I came to . . ."

I didn't even finish before he turned and yelled to the back of the house. "Nan, I need another beer." There was a slight silence, and I was just ready to try again when he yelled, "Now!"

I knew Mrs. Handon's name was Nancy, and I realized he was yelling at her. I felt a knot in my stomach knowing that.

Soon Mrs. Handon came in carrying a beer. She saw me and smiled. "Oh, hi, Mr. Johnson. I didn't know you were here."

I saw this as a good opportunity to say what I wanted to say. "I came to see if I could talk to you and your husband and David and Alex about David and Alex coming to scouts."

Mr. Handon's scowl deepened. He glanced at David, then back at his wife as he spoke. "David can go if he wants. He's already like his mother, and Nan has turned him into a sissy taking him to church and all. But I hoped Alex would grow up to be more like me."

That thought made me shudder. I tried to ignore that feeling as I spoke. "We try hard to make the boys strong and give them skills for survival. And we love to have fathers join us."

Mr. Handon didn't say anything, but just continued to scowl.

Mrs. Handon said, "I think scouting is good for a boy. But perhaps we should ask Alex."

Mr. Handon still didn't say anything. So, David said he would get Alex. A few minutes later, David returned with a boy that looked like a smaller version of himself. Alex had a little more of the blonder hair of his father, and he looked more like his father in other ways, while David looked more like his mother.

Mrs. Handon looked right at Alex as she spoke. "Alex, Mr. Johnson has come to ask you if you would like to go to scouts with David. What do you think?"

I saw Alex's eyes light up, and he nodded vigorously. Then I noticed that he caught sight of his father's scowl. The smile faded from Alex's face. When he spoke, his voice showed a tempered enthusiasm. "Perhaps I could come sometimes."

All eyes turned then to Mr. Handon. He didn't speak, but arose from the couch and went into the other room. No one said anything, and I assumed they knew more about what was happening than I did. Soon, Mr. Handon returned carrying a Smith and Wesson revolver. He sat down and deliberately shoved the beer cans from the coffee table. He laid the revolver down. He then pulled out six bullets one at a time, holding each up, and pointedly inserted them into the gun. When he finished, he cocked the revolver, held it up, and pointed it at me.

"If anything happens to my son, those bullets are for you."

I looked directly at him and didn't flinch. "I'll take that chance. I'm always the last man off the mountain. I will not come off the mountain until each boy has returned safely."

Mr. Handon showed surprise that I didn't cower from him even with a loaded gun pointed at me. Though his scowl deepened, he slowly nodded. David had already turned in his application, but Alex hadn't. Mr. Handon went back to watching his show while Mrs. Handon filled out the form.

When I left, I had all eighteen boys registered and a renewed commitment to always be the last man off the mountain.

4

Rules and Punishments

The scout committee and parents donated lots of things to replenish our burned scout supplies. Harry again took the assignment as the committee chairman. He had learned where his talents were and where they weren't. He now knew he didn't work well with the boys, but he was an organizing genius.

Harry organized the willing parents into a calling tree, where each one had a certain number of others to call. They called all over the community. We soon had new tents and a new cookstove. One man in the community was extremely good at working with wood. He built us a camp box that had shelves for the pots and pans. It had handles so four people could carry it.

Harry had me meet him at the scout storage shed so we could inventory everything. I was pleased with all the gear that had been donated.

"You know what I always find most interesting?" Harry said. "The poor people always donate a lot, and the rich people donate very little."

I laughed. "I've seen it, too. But I wouldn't call them rich, only wealthy. The poor who help others are far richer."

The only things I felt we could use more of were Dutch ovens, so I purchased them with my own money. I felt I could use them for camping with my family, too. Once I had them, I felt like we had all we needed. It was time for our first campout. But there was one thing I knew we needed to do first.

At our scout meeting, I was pleased to see that all eighteen boys were there when I called the meeting to order. After we had done all the preliminaries, like quoting the scout oath and law, I addressed the main issue of the night.

"Okay," I said. "Rod and I may be your scoutmasters, but

it's your troop. We may be the ones that have to deal with certain challenges, but we want you all to have a say in how the troop runs. With both safety and scouting ideals in mind, I want you to determine the rules. Then we'll talk about punishment for anyone who breaks the rules."

Gordy's hand shot up. "Everyone has to do their share and rotate in cooking, cleaning, and everything."

"I'll write it down," I said, marking it on my paper.

"The rules on treating the environment properly means we should not chop down trees unless we absolutely have to, especially green trees," Mort said.

"Are you referring to anything in particular?" I asked.

"Am I, Gordy?" Mort said.

"Why are you asking me?" Gordy replied.

"You're the one who is always chopping down trees," Mort said.

"I better write it down," I said.

The boys came up with lots of rules, including not blowing cans up in the fire, not stealing anyone else's stuff, obeying rules for bear safety, and many others. It took most of our troop time to list the rules they wanted, and when they had exhausted their ideas, I said, "We can always change, add, or delete these as we see necessary. Now comes the harder part. What do we do for punishment if rules are broken?"

"I think the scoutmaster, meaning you, should throw the offender into the creek, river, or lake wherever we are camping. That is, of course, if you think you are tough enough," Gordy said with a bit of a sneer.

Gordy was the biggest scout. He wasn't the oldest, but both of his parents were quite tall, and he had inherited their size. He already stood taller than me and probably had some years of growth left. He also thought he was extremely tough, and I could tell by the tone of his voice that it was not just a suggestion but a bit of a challenge. I was not about to take the bait.

"I suppose I could do that," I replied. "But there are a few problems with it. First, it is not really the scout model for discipline. I am not in this job to hurt anyone in any way. I'm definitely not going to throw anyone into the creek in the winter and endanger their health in the cold. And second, you might think that type of discipline is okay for breaking a safety rule like exploding cans in the fire or for an environmental infraction like chopping down trees, but it doesn't match something minor."

"How about this?" Devin said. "If it's summer, and it's a safety or environmental infraction, you throw the person in the stream. If it is something else, the person picks up an extra chore."

"But that still doesn't deal with it not being a scout model of discipline," I replied.

"You're not scared you won't be able to do it, are you?" Gordy asked with a sarcastic tone.

"Nothing of the sort," I replied.

"If we are the ones choosing it, then shouldn't it be okay scout discipline?" Mort asked.

I thought about it and then turned to Rod. "What do you think, Rod?"

He shrugged. "I think it's okay. That was the way my father did discipline."

"Okay," I said. "I don't really like it, but I'll make you a deal. If an infraction is severe enough that you feel such a disciplinary measure is appropriate, then I will carry it out as you have chosen, but only on a couple of conditions. First, as I have said, it doesn't endanger or hurt anyone. That includes not throwing anyone in the water from September through May when it is cold. And second, you boys must unanimously vote that is the punishment to be carried out. That means everyone, and I mean everyone, including the boy who is being punished, has to agree to it and feel it's just. If he disagrees with it, he will have the right to opt for another punishment, like more chores or something. And no one is to pressure him into accepting it."

"I would rather be thrown in the lake and get the punishment over with than have more chores," Mort said.

"I would, too," Gordy added. "That is, if the person throwing me in thinks they are tough enough to actually do it."

"Okay," I replied. "But before we take a vote on this, there is one more thing I will insist on. I will not even take a vote on that type of punishment until I have talked to the boy who is to be punished. If he doesn't agree to it, I will not even put him through the vote. I do not want to embarrass him."

"That's good," Jason said.

"Does everyone agree with this rule as we have set it out?" I asked.

All raised their hands.

"Because I don't want to hurt, embarrass, or in any other way cause problems for any of you," I said, "if any of you ever have a problem with any of our rules, please talk to me privately, and I will keep it between you and me."

They all said they would. I wrote down what we agreed upon. And we moved to the next item. They suggested a few more punishments related to different things, and I wrote them down.

I asked by a show of hands if everyone agreed, and all raised their hands.

"All right, then," I said. "I will write up what we have decided on and make a copy for each of us to sign next week. Next week, we will also plan our first campout. Now I think we should go play some basketball."

"I have one question," Sam said. "What if you or Rod break a rule? Who is going to punish you?"

"Yeah, that's a good point," Devan said. "We never said what would happen if leaders break the rules."

"That really is a good point," I replied. "What do you suggest?"

Gordy laughed. "Leaders should have the same punishments we have."

"I could live with that," I replied. "But does that mean I throw myself in the lake?"

The boys laughed, and I could tell they thought that sounded stupid.

"We will throw you and Rod in the lake if you need it," Gordy said.

"Do I just let you, or do I take you all in with me?" I asked.

Gordy laughed. "Like that would happen. There are eighteen of us and only one of you."

"Well, I'll tell you what," I said. "If I deserve it, I promise I will go in the lake one way or the other."

The boys turned and looked at Rod.

He shrugged. "And I'll think about it," he said.

After the boys headed to the church gym for basketball, Rod laughed. "You do realize that most of that discussion about punishments was preparation for a challenge against you, don't you? You know that, eventually, they will try to throw you in a stream or lake or something, don't you?"

"Oh, I realize it," I replied. "I saw it with Harry, and I will have to watch my back. But I think the challenge will come sooner or later. It's better that when it comes, there are rules, and they are the ones who made them. That way, they can't complain about the outcome."

Rod really chuckled at that. "Do you think that any of them know you were a state champion wrestler?"

"No. But I don't think it will be long before they find out."

Having the rules and punishments out of the way, we played a rousing game of lightning. I found out my shooting skills in basketball were lacking, especially when I tried to hurry. I wasn't too bad if I slowed down and took my time. When we finished, and the parents came to pick up their sons, the boys were happy.

*****

The following week, I had the commitment for them to sign. I read it as the boys followed along, and then they signed it. Rod and I also signed a copy so the boys would know we had committed to the same things. We all then settled down to plan our campout.

Because it was late March, the ice wouldn't be thick enough to trust it to go ice fishing. And there was still snow, especially in the high country, so we couldn't go too far off the main roads. We decided we would go to Porcupine Creek. There was a nice year-round stream there, and a hillside where the boys could do a bit of sledding. Someone had also put up a rope swing between two trees. I had been there often with my family, and the swing from down off the hillside was always a favorite.

We talked about the food and decided what we would eat. I asked for volunteers who needed a cooking merit badge to help me work on the food, and Devin and Dallin still needed theirs. They volunteered to go with me to buy the food and direct the cooking on the campout. I handed out a checklist for each of the boys listing what they should bring to be sufficiently warm and prepared for an early spring campout.

When we finished planning, we played an intense game of basketball.

5
First Campout

Everything for the campout went pretty much as planned. Later in the week, I picked up Devin and Dallin, and we went and bought the food using part of the scout budget allocated to us by the committee. On Friday, as soon as I could get off work, I loaded my gear that I had prepared the night before, along with my Dutch ovens, and headed to the church. Most of the boys were already there. Marissa was there, waiting for me.

"Are you sure he won't freeze to death?" she asked.

"Did he pack all the things I had on the checklist?" I asked.

"Yes."

"Then he'll be fine. I will make sure of it."

It was about all Sam could do to get his mother to leave him and head back home. This was his first campout with the boys, and I was sure his excitement alone would keep him warm.

The vehicles were nearly loaded up when David and Alex came. Their father was driving, and as he pulled into the parking lot, the car weaving back and forth, I was sure he must be drunk. As they climbed from the vehicle, Mr. Handon yelled out his window. "Have fun at sissy scouts."

David rolled his eyes, but Alex looked down and couldn't face anyone in his embarrassment. As Mr. Handon headed out of the parking lot, he drove onto the sidewalk and nearly hit Gordy. Mr. Handon hit the horn and kept it blaring for about a half mile down the road.

"Hey!" Gordy yelled after him. "This is a sidewalk, and I was walking here!" He then turned to David and Alex. "What is it with your dad?"

"Just ignore him," David said.

"He's really a good guy when he's not drunk," Alex added.

I felt sorry for them, especially for Alex. I could tell he loved and admired his father, and it bothered him when his father did those kinds of things. David, it seemed, was much more used to it and just ignored it.

We finished loading the gear into my van and Rod's pickup, had a prayer for safety, and we were on our way. My big fifteen-passenger van hauled most of the boys, but Gordy, Justin, Mort, and Dallin all squeezed in Rod's truck with him.

I knew it would be nearly dark when we arrived at our camp, so I had prepared fajitas ahead of time. I had a bag of precooked chicken and one full of all sorts of vegetables. While the others set up their tents, I got a fire going and put the vegetables in a pan to sauté. Dallin and Devin joined me to cook once their tents were ready.

By the time the camp was totally set up, the vegetables were cooked, and we tossed in the chicken. After stirring in the meat, the food was ready in about ten minutes. We pulled out some salsa, and I heated some tortilla shells. The boys were hungry, and the food went fast. While they ate, I put some oil in a Dutch oven and set it on the fire. By the time the boys finished the fajitas, the oil was sizzling, and I started cooking scones. My wife, Hannah, had made the bread dough. The scones were delicious slathered in Hannah's honey butter. The boys ate until they could hardly waddle around the camp.

When they were done, Rod and I sat down and ate what was left, but it was enough. Everyone sat on logs around the campfire and enjoyed the warmth and visiting. As is usually the case at that time of year, the night sky was beautiful. I had studied some about the stars and was able to point out a few of the constellations.

"When you look up at the big sky with all the stars, don't you feel kind of small?" Mort asked.

"In some ways," I replied. "But I think about the fact that He who made all of that made me, and it makes me feel a bit more important, especially when the scriptures tell us He is our father."

It was late when the boys finally all went to bed. Rod and I stayed up for a little while, enjoying the peace and quiet. I thought about the big assignment he and I had taken on to help these boys become honorable young men. That made me feel less adequate than all the stars of the heavens could.

I checked and made sure all the boys had plenty of blankets. I brought extras. My wonderful wife made lots of them for our home and was good to let me bring them. Once they were all set in their tents, Rod and I retired to ours. I lay awake for quite a while, still thinking about each boy and the challenges they faced.

*****

The sun wasn't even up yet when I heard two boys get up to answer nature's call. They hurried back to their warm beds, but I knew it would be a good time for me to get up and start a fire.

I shivered as I slipped into my cold clothes and climbed out of the tent. There was frost on the outside of the tents and on the vehicle windows. It was a bit of a challenge to get a fire going, but soon it was crackling and popping pleasantly. I filled a pan with water and put it on the fire to heat for hot chocolate.

Rod soon joined me, and as a few boys started wandering out to warm themselves by the fire, I told Dallin and Devin that I needed them to help me cook so they could count it on their  merit badge. They reluctantly came, and soon we had bacon, eggs, and pancakes frying. I taught them to put a little bacon on the edge of each griddle and use the grease from it to coat the pan between batches of food to keep it from sticking.

We had four griddles going, but the boys ate the food as fast as it came off. No one complained, however, because they could enjoy the hot chocolate between helpings. Steven and Tanner had the assignment for cleanup, and after we finished breakfast, they reluctantly helped while the other boys headed off to do a little sledding. As we were getting toward the end of the cleanup, I shooed them off to join the others while I finished.

Meanwhile, Rod was showing the younger boys some techniques for winter survival. "How did you build the fire?" this morning, he asked me.

"Just like I normally do," I replied. "I used a little paper and some dry wood."

"How did you keep it dry with the frost?" he asked.

"I put some in my van last night."

"That," he said to the boys, "is good thinking ahead. But here is another thing I do."

He brought out a bucket. When I looked in it, I asked, "Is that sawdust?"

"Yes, but not just sawdust," he replied. "I soaked it in diesel. Diesel isn't as flammable as gas, so it isn't dangerous, but it lights easily and burns well."

We took some of the mix to another campfire spot, put in some of his diesel-soaked sawdust with some paper under it, put some wood on top, and lit it. The minute the flame touched the sawdust, it started to burn easily, but not violently like it would with gas.

"I like that," I said. "I've learned something new, too."

Just then, we heard someone saying, "No! No! No!" We turned and could see Sam down on his belly. He had apparently laid down on his stomach on the hill next to the stream and was inching toward it to fill his canteen. But the bank was steep and slick, and he started to slide. At just the last moment, he screamed as he plunged headfirst into the icy water.

In an instant, I was at the stream, jumped in, and pulled him out. The cold water bit into me like thorns. I pulled him out onto the bank.

I hurried him to his tent, and since we didn't have any big towels, not expecting anyone to go swimming, I handed him a blanket. "Take off your wet clothes, dry off with this blanket, and then get some dry clothes on. Wrap up in a dry blanket and get out here by the fire as quickly as you can."

I asked Rod to put some more water on for hot chocolate, and then I went to my tent and did the same thing I had told Sam to do. Soon the two of us were in dry clothes, wrapped in blankets, shivering by the fire. It wasn't long before we stopped shivering and were feeling better. Mort hung our clothes up on a line over the fire to dry, but unfortunately, his line wasn't tied tight enough, and it drooped, singeing the bottom of both Sam's and my clothes.

At about noon, our clothes were dry enough, and Sam and I both changed back into them since they were warmer than what we had on. I had just finished changing when I heard the chopping. The other boys followed me to the sound, and, of course, we found Gordy chopping on a tree.

"Gordy, what are you doing?" I asked.

"Chopping this dead tree," he said with a grin.

"What makes you think it's dead?" I asked.

"It doesn't have leaves," he replied.

"For your information," I said, "it's March, and deciduous trees don't leaf out until late April or May."

"Well, I guess you will have to try to throw me in the creek," he said with a challenge in his voice.

"Do you remember the commitment you signed said I wouldn't do that in the winter, meaning September through May?" I asked. "If it were summer, and the troop voted on it, I would do it. But right now, you get to do camp cleanup."

The smile disappeared from his face. "That's not fair."

"You signed the commitment," I said. I then turned to the others. "All in favor of Gordy doing camp cleanup, raise your hand." Everyone except for Gordy raised their hand. "All opposed," I said. Gordy raised his hand. "Well, Gordy, I guess you got it."

"That's not fair," Gordy said. "It's summer."

I laughed. "Summer doesn't have snow. We will use summer discipline rules when it's June through August, the snow is gone, and the days are over fifty degrees."

"You also said it had to be unanimous," Gordy said.

"The paper said it had to be unanimous to throw someone in the stream," I replied. "That doesn't hold for kitchen duty."

Gordy scowled but did his assignment. I was counting on peer pressure to help keep the troop in order, and so far, so good.

I helped Gordy clean up and soon let him go back to sledding. "But no more tree chopping," I said.

At about mid-afternoon, we loaded back into the vehicles and headed home. As I drove, most of the boys fell asleep. When we arrived at the church, Marissa was waiting to pick up Sam. When she saw his scorched clothes, her eyes grew wide. "What happened?"

"I fell in the creek," Sam answered enthusiastically.

"What?" Marissa gasped. "In the winter?"

"Yeah," Mort added with a laugh. "You should have seen it. Sam looked like an otter sliding down the snowy bank into the creek."

"Yeah," Gordy chimed in, turning to Sam. "You otter be more careful, Sam."

The boys all started clamoring to tell some of the story, including how we got Sam in dry clothes, then put his others over the fire, and how they got singed. I could see by the expression on Marissa's face that the more they talked, the worse it was. Finally, she turned to me and just blurted out, "You let my son fall in a freezing cold creek?"

"It's okay, Mom," Sam said. "Tom jumped in after me and pulled me out."

She looked at me, and her expression softened slightly. "You jumped into a freezing stream to pull my son out."

"I told you I would take care of him," I said. "And after that accident, I was able to teach him and the other boy some important survival skills about getting dry and warm immediately."

Marissa paused and then said, "I don't know whether to hug you or to slap you."

"How about we compromise on a handshake?" I replied.

"Oh, Mom," Sam said, his enthusiasm not damped in the least, "it was the greatest time ever. And you should try Tom's fajitas and scones."

With that, Sam joined the other boys, who had headed off to unload the camp equipment. Marissa stared at me for a moment, took a deep breath, and then turned and walked away. As for me, I just smiled, thinking of Sam's words. "It was the greatest time ever!"

6

Government Markers and Ghost Stories

The evening of our next campout was late in April, and it was beautiful as we pulled into the campsite in Kilgore. The boy scouts' goal is to have one camp-out each month, and I hoped to do that as much as possible. The boys had voted to camp on West Camas Creek. It's a remote area, yet still quite accessible, and fishing was already open there, where it wasn't in most places until the Saturday before Memorial Day.

After Sam's trip into the stream on the previous camp-out, I wasn't sure Marissa would let him come, but she brought him. She did hug him a little extra, which embarrassed him, but he was willing to put up with it to be able to go with us.

With the weather being warmer, I brought my two sons, who were six and eight years old. It would be a good chance to spend some time with them. Rod had also brought his oldest son, who was in age right between mine.

The days were getting longer, and daylight savings made it so we still had quite a few hours of light after arriving at our camp. For dinner, the boys had voted to bring their own tinfoil dinner so that they could put them into the coals of the fire and spend their time fishing. While they set up their tents, I got a nice fire going, and by the time the camp was ready, there were beautiful white coals, perfect for cooking.

The boys put their dinners in the coals and were soon off to the stream. Sam had never been fishing before, and Rod was good to show him the proper way to bait his hook and the best places for fish to hide in the stream. Rod could get his hook to drift perfectly into the best eddies and pools, and he pulled in fish after fish, while Sam mostly caught sticks.

Sam was growing frustrated, but when he finally caught his

39

first fish, the annoyance of all the branches he had hooked was quickly forgotten.

I continued to turn the tinfoil dinners, and by the time the sun dropped below the horizon on the western sky, the food was ready, and the boys gathered around the campfire. As they did, some of them sniffed the air.

"What is that horrible smell?" Devin asked.

I shrugged. It smells like it is coming from the fire. But I kept turning the meals, so I don't think it is from burning. It must be something someone brought.

As the boys started opening their dinners, we found the source of the smell. Sam's mother didn't quite get the concept of a tinfoil dinner and thought she was packing a lunch. She had put two peanut butter and jelly sandwiches inside his tinfoil, along with a plastic container full of Jell-O. Sam hadn't looked to see what was inside before putting it in the fire, so when he opened it up, the sandwiches were charcoal, and the plastic container was liquified all around them. They were all one big mass of stinky burnt plastic.

"It is so well wrapped in plastic; maybe you should have it mounted to put on your bedroom wall," Dallin said.

Sam didn't think that was funny since he didn't have any dinner. The other boys were willing to share their vegetables with Sam, and he ate a little, but when he found out I had brought bread for scones, he was willing to wait.

As we ate, we looked at the beautiful western sky painted in red and orange hues. We had a few good fish that I fried as the boys ate. I added some steak seasoning, and even boys who said they didn't like fish liked it.

The boys spent more time trading parts of their dinner than eating them. Most of the boys had some meat wrapped in potatoes. If their mother helped them, there were also vegetables like carrots and onions. Everyone tried to trade their vegetables for the meat from someone else's dinner.

I pulled out my tinfoil dinner and opened it. Hannah had cooked up some steak, basted in a special teriyaki sauce she had made. The aroma quickly drew all the boys around.

"Wow!" Gordy said. "That smells great! What is it?"

"It's teriyaki steak. My wife makes it for me because she knows how much I like it."

"Can I try a bite?" he asked.

I knew once I started, that would be the end of my dinner, but I decided to share anyway. I split the meat into four parts. One was for each of my sons, one was to share, and the fourth was for Sam.

Sam was happy to have a share and devoured it. While my sons ate theirs, I cut the fourth portion into bite-size pieces and let everyone have a taste. They liked it a lot and became like a wolf pack prowling around to see if there was anything left. I only saved one bite for myself and almost wished I hadn't because it just made me wish I had more.

But after I started cooking scones, the meat was soon forgotten as the boys slathered on the honey butter and jam. Hannah's honey butter was especially popular.

"What makes the honey butter so good?" David asked.

"It's her secret ingredient," I replied.

The boys all guessed what they thought it was, but none did. I finally told them.

"She adds a good portion of marshmallow cream."

Rod laughed. "That would make anything good."

I cooked piles of scones but barely got enough to feel somewhat satisfied, even though I cooked more than I had at the previous campout.

As soon as the boys were full, the younger ones wandered off into the dark to play a moonlight game of steal the flag. I had brought marshmallows for my sons, and we shared them with Rod's son, along with the scouts that might come wandering by and wanted to cook one.

We were still finishing eating when I heard the familiar chop, chop, and knew Gordy was attacking a tree again. I could tell by the noise that it wasn't a little hatchet he was using this time. It was an ax. Dallin and Devin came walking into camp from that direction.

"Is Gordy chopping down a green tree again?" I asked them.

Devin shook his head. "It's actually a dry one this time."

"But is it a standing tree?" I asked. "Our rules are that we don't chop any standing tree."

Dallin nodded. "Yes, it is a standing tree. It's not huge, only about six inches in diameter, but it's ugly with lots of short, stubby branches."

"So what do we do about it?" I asked.

Suddenly, Gordy screamed and started shouting, "No, no, no, no, no!"

We ran toward where he was, not too far away. The sun was completely down, and there was little more than moonlight to see. When we got close enough to tell what was happening, I could see the tree slowly leaning toward a tent.

"Not on our tent, you idiot!" Mort yelled.

Both Mort and Gordy ran toward their tent, and the tree continued to lean farther and farther. I ran for the two boys. They reached their tent just as the tree popped. I reached them at the same instant and jerked them out of the way of the falling tree. I jumped to get clear of it, too, but I felt a sharp pain in my leg. It all happened so fast that I didn't have time to think about it.

When the dry tree hit the ground, it exploded. Pieces of wood, tent, and sleeping bags flew in all directions. For an instant, I couldn't see anything from the dust and falling debris. When it cleared, the tent and its contents were strewn in pieces all around. But Gordy and Mort were safe.

Mort got right up in Gordy's face. "What do you think you were doing dropping the tree on my stuff?"

"It was my stuff, too," Gordy huffed.

"I don't care about your stuff," Mort said. "You deserve to have it ruined. But I didn't chop the tree."

Rod went to get a flashlight while I stopped what was getting close to a fight.

I got between Mort and Gordy. "Okay, guys. Arguing won't help anything.

Rod returned with the flashlight and shined it on the mess. There wasn't much left of the tent or the sleeping bags.

"We can clean this up in the morning when we have more light," I said. "As for tonight, I have some extra blankets. You can see if someone else has some room in their tents, or you can sleep in the vehicles."

They chose to sleep in the vehicles, one in each. Mort was not about to sleep in the same car as "Stupid Gordy," and Gordy wasn't keen on being in the same one as Mort.

We had just gotten that settled when Rod turned his light on me.

"Tom, you're bleeding horribly."

Everyone turned to look at me, and I looked down at my leg. A branch must have hit me because my pant leg was ripped wide open, and blood flowed out of it. I took a knife and cut the hem of the pant leg so I could open it. I had a nasty gash.

"And that's your fault, too, Gordy," Mort said.

"Okay," I said. "It doesn't matter. We're all safe, and this is nothing we can't bandage."

We returned to the fire where we would have more light, and Devin retrieved the first-aid kit from my van. He set it down and opened it up.

"Hand me a swab and some alcohol," Rod said.

Before Devin could, Sam grabbed it. "Here, let me."

Before anyone could stop him, he poured a good amount of it on my wound. I let out a yelp.

"You swab it on," Rod said. "Not try to drown it."

As I was panting from the pain, I said, "I think it's time we have a good lesson on first-aid."

I spent some time going over wound care. I wrapped my wound carefully, showing how to keep the items clean and the wound disinfected. I then had them practice on each other. We had tried to do some first aid at the evening scout meetings, but they paid little or no attention. Now, with an accident in the camp, they seemed more willing to learn.

As they practiced the bandaging, Mort said, "Can I wound Gordy and make him bleed so it's realistic?"

"You and what army?" Gordy replied.

"One person bleeding is sufficient," Rod said.

When we finished the first aid lesson, we all gathered around the fire. Gordy seemed a bit humbled, knowing the accident was his fault. He sat down beside me.

"Hey, sorry about dropping that tree and getting you hurt."

I patted his shoulder. "We have rules for many reasons, Gordy, but one of the main ones is to keep everyone safe. Imagine how you would feel if Mort had been in the tent. I'm just glad no one was hurt!"

Rod laughed. "No one?"

"Well, not badly," I said. "I'll be okay."

"What about Gordy's punishment for breaking the rules?" Devin asked.

"I think Gordy punished himself when all of his things were destroyed," I replied.

"What about my things?" Mort asked.

Gordy, still humbled by the evening's events, said, "I'll replace your sleeping bag."

"You know guys," I said, "this brings up a good point. Often in life, when we do something wrong, it eventually brings its own punishment. It isn't usually as fast as this was tonight, but it's almost impossible to do something wrong without it catching up to you eventually."

I turned to Rod. "Rod, do you have anything you want to add?"

He smiled. "I will just say amen to that. I have done plenty of stupid things in my life, and they eventually come back to bite me. Sometimes it can be just that your children do the same thing you did, and you feel like a hypocrite telling them not to, especially when what you did was worse."

"Did you guys really do stupid things when you were our age?" Sam asked.

"Of course we did," I replied.

"Why don't you guys ever talk about them?" Seth asked.

I laughed. "Because you do enough on your own. You don't need any more ideas."

Rod chuckled. "I thought you were a perfect kid, Tom."

I laughed. "I had my moments."

We had a good talk; then the boys decided they wanted to play a game of steal-the-flag before it got too late.

"Okay," I said. "But there are a couple of conditions. You must stay in two's, always know where your partner is, and stay within fifty yards of the camp. You must come to camp immediately if we call."

"Why?" David asked.

"Where it is spring, bears will be coming out of hibernation and be hungry. We are not deep into bear country, but we are on the edge of it. There shouldn't be any problem, but we don't want to take chances."

They all agreed and went off. Soon I could hear the boys scurrying around, calling to each other, and trying unsuccessfully to mimic all sorts of animal sounds. Every half hour, I called out, and the boys immediately came to camp. After making sure everyone was safe, I would let them go back out for a while.

Eventually, I heard a lot of commotion, some of them yelling, calling to each other to "come see what we found."

I was just about ready to go see what was going on when they came into camp dragging something and laid it near the fire.

"Look what we found!" Tanner exclaimed.

It was a big cement post. It had a bronze marker on it. Brushing away the dirt, I read the inscription. "Government survey marker. Do not remove on penalty of $5000 fine, one year in jail, or both."

"Where did you get this?" I asked.

"Oh, can you believe somebody just left it half-buried in the woods?" Mort answered.

I told them we had to put it back, but they thought they ought to take it home and put it in the scout closet; that way, they could show it off to everyone.

I could just imagine what the scout committee would say when they saw it there; that is, if they could see it among all the other junk. I couldn't convince the boys it belonged to the government no matter what it said, but I also obviously couldn't let them take it home. I looked to Rod for suggestions. He could see my dilemma and just smiled and shrugged. Suddenly, I had an idea.

"Hey guys," I said, "do you like ghost stories?'

"What has that got to do with the cement marker?" Mort asked.

"It's just that it's about time for bed, and when I was young, we often told ghost stories before bed. Besides, that marker reminds me of something I heard about this area where we are camping."

"What if we don't plan to go to bed?" Gordy asked. "Maybe we will play steal the flag all night."

"All the more reason we should tell ghost stories now before we get too tired," I replied.

They agreed, and soon they were gathered around the fire.

I was creating one in my mind for what I wanted when Dexter said, "I got a good one. Can I go first?"

"All right," I said. "Go for it."

Everybody turned their attention to Dexter.

"Okay, so there was this guy who asked out this girl."

"It wasn't you, was it?" Gordy asked. "I'm sure if it was, she would just say no."

"Let him tell the story," Rod said.

"So, he asks her out," Dexter said, continuing. "He takes her to the woods. . . Um, no, I think he took her up on the mountain. No, come to think of it, I think it was the woods."

"Okay, okay," Justin said. "He took her somewhere."

"Yes," Dexter said, "he did. Then when they got there, the girl said, 'Did you know that there is an escaped convict on the loose?' The boy shook his head."

Dexter stopped and looked at the ground for a minute. "Actually, now that I think about it, I think the guy wasn't an escaped convict. He had escaped from the insane asylum."

"Oh, for heaven's sake," Mort said. "Have you ever told a story before?"

I felt sorry for Dexter, so I thought I'd help. "I think I've heard this story. He was a crazy murderer, so he was both a convict and had spent time in the insane asylum."

"Yeah. That's it," Dexter said.

"Tom, why don't you tell it?" Gordy asked. "Maybe that way, it would make sense."

"No," I replied. "Dexter's telling it."

"No, you go ahead," Dexter said. "I can't remember any more, anyway."

"You start to tell us a ghost story and can't remember the ending?" Devin asked. "Now that is crazy."

"Okay," I said. "Sometimes it's hard to remember. But let me tell you what happened. The guy and the girl went out on their date and drove a long way from home. Then they stopped to look at the stars."

"Sure they did," Gordy said.

I continued. "While they were looking at the stars, the girl mentioned this crazy murderer who had escaped. 'And to add to it, he only has one hand,' the girl said. 'The other hand was a hook.' The girl then suggested that they ought to get back to town.

"The boy laughed. 'Why would he be out here?' he asked.

"Just then, there was a sound outside, like someone dragging their fingernails on a chalkboard. But it was coming from along the side of the car."

I continued to make the story up as I went, piecing together stories I had heard from my scout days. I knew I had the boys with me, and by the time I finished with the frightened couple fleeing back to town only to find a hook on the car's bumper, I was sure there was not a boy that would sleep all night.

"That was scary," Sam said.

"Yeah," I replied. "But not as scary as the one I heard about right here where we're camped."

"What was that?" Jason asked, trying to sound brave.

"You know that cement post you guys pulled out that had a government marker on it? It could be a government marker. But have you ever stopped to think that out here in the middle of nowhere, it could be an alien beacon disguised as a government marker?"

"What are you saying?" Sam asked.

"Think about it, guys. Maybe aliens left it, and by pulling it out, you have launched a spaceship to this very spot to pick up specimens to take back to their planet."

If I had their attention on the last story, it was nothing like now when what I was saying pertained to the activities of the evening. Besides, they might not believe the cement post was a government marker, but an alien beacon was plausible.

"But we pulled it out hours ago," Dallin said. "They would have been here by now."

"Hey, give them time," I said. "They might live a few thousand light years away. They might not get here until tomorrow."

"Yeah," Justin said. "They might be driving a Chevy spaceship, in which case they could be a lot longer than that."

"Or," retorted Mort, "They might be driving a Ford and broke down somewhere in the middle of space."

"That would be because the Chevy ones. . ."

The best type of pickup was often an area of disagreement, and I decided it would be good to cut it short. I also thought it might not be a good idea to mention that I drive a Toyota.

"Did you guys want me to tell you the rest of the story?" I asked. They nodded, so I continued.

"It doesn't really matter what kind of spaceship it was, but what matters is that the first appearance of one was probably over a century ago. And I should tell you why I have the concerns I do."

They all leaned in toward me as I continued. "Once, over a hundred years ago, there lived in these parts a beautiful young girl who was about twelve years old. She liked to wander in the forest. Then, one day, she found what she described as a cement pillar. When she touched it, a bright light flashed. It was seen by people for miles around. Everyone rushed to the spot, but when they got there, the light was gone, and so was the girl. However, there was a dark circle burned in the grass."

"Kind of like when Jason was in charge of the fire, huh?" Chester asked.

"Hey, that only happened once," Jason replied.

I ignored them and continued with the story. "About a week later, an old woman who was around eighty years old appeared and claimed to be the girl.

She said she had lived on a far-off planet for decades but had somehow escaped and returned through a time warp. Thus, even though she had lived for years on the other planet, the time warp had brought her back to almost the same time as when she had left."

Far in the distance, interrupting my story, we heard a mountain lion scream. I thought, what perfect timing! I seized on the opportunity as I continued.

"Sometimes, when the moon is exactly right, you can hear her cry. She isn't quite human and can never die, and she knows someday the aliens will return for her. So, she wanders these lands and screams at the life she lost, waiting to catch someone she can send in her place."

Again, the mountain lion screamed. "What was that?!" Jason said, jumping to his feet.

"That," Gordy said, rolling his eyes, "was a whole bunch of poppycock."

Just about then, a coyote howled. Another one answered back.

"You know," I said. "That coyote howl reminds me of something the old woman claimed to have said. She said that the aliens could take different shapes and often disguise themselves as wild animals, especially coyotes. When I see or hear a coyote, it makes me wonder if that is really what it is."

"I really got to go," Jeremy said. "Who would like to go with me?"

No one else seemed to have to, though some were squirming. I asked him why he didn't just go by himself. He told me he didn't have a flashlight. I tossed him mine. He looked at it nervously, then went barely out of sight. Suddenly, we heard a noise behind the tent.

"Hey!" Dallin yelled. "That's my tent! You better not be doing what I think you're doing!"

Almost instantly, Jeremy returned with a relieved smile on his face.

"Well," I said, "maybe we ought to put the marker back tomorrow."

The boys all nodded their agreement.

Rod looked at me and grinned. "Hopefully, it won't be too

late."

I stood and yawned. "Maybe we should put the fire out and head to bed. That is, unless you guys are planning on playing more steal the flag. Just watch out for the coyotes if you do."

"You know, I'm feeling kind of tired," Gordy said. "Maybe we should go to bed."

All the other boys agreed, and soon they were all in their tents, except for Gordy and Mort, who were in the vehicles. My boys also went to bed, and so did Rod's. I sat back down by the fire, and Rod looked over at me and smiled.

"An alien space marker? That is about the biggest bunch of bull I've ever heard. Where did you get all that?"

"I made it up. And they believed it, didn't they? And they agreed to put the marker back tomorrow. Besides, they aren't staying up all night."

He laughed. "Yeah, but how many of them are actually going to sleep? And do you know what that means? That means we won't get any sleep either."

"That might be true," I said. "But I doubt we will have to worry about them wandering off."

I went to my tent with my boys and stretched out on my sleeping bag to sleep. Actually, calling it a sleeping bag is a misnomer. A person never really sleeps in them unless they've hiked all day, and then they could sleep on top of a cactus. What a person really does is lay there until they get so stiff they can't move. A better name would be a lay-awake-all-night bag, especially when the boys in the tents around you keep their flashlights on all night.

*****

Rod was right. It was a long night. At the slightest sound of a coyote or anything else, I'd hear a voice say, "What was that?" Some boys who kept their flashlights on all night found their batteries dead the next morning. I think the boys all eventually fell asleep from sheer exhaustion at about two in the morning.

The following day, when I got up and climbed out of my tent, I wasn't too surprised to see that the boys had all pulled their tents closer around the fire pit.

I got a fire going and put some water on for hot chocolate.

When Gordy came wandering up, he laughed. "What's all this with the tents so close to the fire? Did you guys get scared from the stupid ghost story?"

"It got cold, and we decided to get closer to the fire," Sam said.

"Yeah, right," Gordy smirked. "The fire was out."

"This from a guy who slept inside a pickup," Devin said.

"I slept in the pickup because my tent was trashed," Gordy snapped.

"You could have slept out on the ground," Jason said.

I thought this was a good place to end this conversation. "Hey guys, I don't know about you, but I'm hungry. And I thought you wanted to get fishing. What say we get some breakfast?"

They gathered around and filled their cups with hot chocolate while I got pancakes cooking. Chester and Jeremy were assigned to help with breakfast, and they joined me. As soon as breakfast was over, we carried the marker back to where they said they had found it. We carefully slid it into its hole and put the dirt around it. The boys teased each other about being scared of aliens, but I noticed that no one wandered too far from camp to fish.

At about noon, we all loaded up to go home. When we arrived back at the church, Marissa hugged Sam like she hadn't seen him in years.

"How was it?" she asked as he pulled away in embarrassment.

"Mom, I caught a fish. Tom saved Gordy and Mort from a falling tree. Tom and Rod taught us first aid to bandage Tom's leg. Tom told ghost stories about aliens and coyotes. We heard coyotes and mountain lions. Oh, Mom! It was the best camp-out ever!"

As Sam told each part, I could see Marissa's eyes grow wider. When Sam finished, Marissa looked at me. She glanced down at my torn pants, covered in dry blood. Her eyes raised to meet mine. When I looked into her eyes, I could almost read her thoughts.

"And we're all home safe and sound," I said.

Marissa smiled a slight smile and nodded. "Yes, everyone is home safe and sound."

7

Hiking and Fishing

When the boys settled down enough for the scout meeting to plan our next campout, some things quickly became apparent. Fishing was one of the key things they wanted to do.

"Fishing still isn't open in some areas until Memorial Day," Rod said. "I know we went to Camas Creek last month, but Camas Creek is open for year-round fishing. I'd already been there this spring and knew the fishing was fairly good. Maybe we could just go further up on West Camas Creek."

The boys all voted that they would like to go there.

"Could we do a little hiking while we're there?" Sam asked.

"If we camp at the top end of West Camas Creek," Rod said, "there is a nice campsite right across from Castle Peak. We could hike that."

"Only after fishing," Gordy said.

We decided everyone would fish until around ten o'clock, and then we'd start on the hike. That meant we would have to have sandwiches for lunch. The boys said they wanted to eat lunch at the top of Castle Peak.

As the boys headed off for basketball, Rod and I finished up before joining them. "I'm not familiar with Castle Peak," I said. "What kind of hike should we prepare for?"

"It's a ridge on the continental divide," Rod explained. "It isn't a long hike, only a mile or two. But the top part turns quite steep and has rocks you wind your way through that look like a castle's walls. That's where it gets its name."

That sounded like a perfect hike. Rod and I finished our work and joined the boys for basketball.

When the weekend came for our campout, I purchased the food on Thursday after work. The boys had voted to have hamburgers in the evening and French toast for breakfast. It was Sam and Seth's turn to work on the cooking merit badge, so I picked them up to help get the food. Sam talked about how much he loved scouting and how glad he was that his mother let him go with us.

At one point, he turned to me. "You know, Tom, she says the only reason she lets me go on campouts in the cold is because she trusts you."

"I hope I always live worthy of that trust," I said.

When we met for the campout the next day, a slight rain had started. "Does everyone have their rain gear?" I asked as we prepared to leave.

A couple of boys didn't have raincoats, so we made sure we had extra garbage bags to fashion them some. After a quick prayer, we were on our way.

As we got close to our destination, the rain increased. Rod led the way. He knew the camping in that area better than I did. When we pulled into the camp, I told the boys that the first order of business was to get their tents set up.

"Make sure you dig small trenches around your tents to drain the water away like we have talked about," I said.

We made sure everyone was equipped with a raincoat or a garbage bag to keep them dry, then sent them to work. I was able to get a fire going with the wood I had put under the backseat of my van. I got water boiling for hot chocolate and hamburgers cooking on the griddles, but I struggled to keep the griddles hot enough. The pouring rain cooled the grills and made cooking challenging.

Once the tents were up, I had the boys get hamburgers ready, minus the meat. They then climbed into their tents to stay dry. I told Sam and Seth I would have them cook dinner on another day so they could stay dry in their tents. I cooked the meat while Rod held an umbrella over the grills. When the meat was ready, Rod and I took it to the boys in their tents, then began cooking more. It took a long time, but eventually, everyone was satisfied.

As the sun's glimmer behind the clouds disappeared below the edge of the horizon, the rain finally stopped. Everyone got a hot chocolate and gathered around the fire. I had brought bread dough, as always, for scones, and I thought this would be a good time to cook them.

After I started cooking, Seth said, "Tom, tell us a story."

The boys all nodded their agreement, so I pondered what story I should tell. Finally, I thought of something.

"If I am going to tell you a story tonight, I think I want to tell you a scout one and not a ghost story."

I then told them the following story.

*****

When I was younger, there was a man, Fred, whom I admired. He always did good things. If a widow needed food, he was always the first to take some over. He was always the first to volunteer if there was a community project to help older people get wood in for winter. One day, when I asked Fred why he was always helping people, he told me his story.

Fred said he grew up in a tough part of town. He ran with the wrong crowd, and it looked like he was destined to be deeply involved with a dangerous gang. Fred said he refused to go to church when his mother asked and spent his time instead stealing and doing things that were wrong.

56

Fred said he spent some time in juvenile lockup. He knew it broke his mother's heart, but he didn't care. He was going to live his life as he wanted, and nothing was going to change that. More than once, his mother spent what little she had to get him out of jail or out of trouble, and he never even appreciated it.

When Fred turned twelve, he said the scoutmaster came to him and asked him if he wanted to be part of the troop. He told the scoutmaster he wasn't the slightest bit interested. Scouting was stupid, and going around doing good all the time really got a person nowhere. He shut the door in the scoutmaster's face.

One day, the scoutmaster showed up and asked Fred if he wanted to go fishing. Fred said he jumped at the chance. His father had disappeared when he was young, leaving Fred and his mother alone. He loved out-of-doors things and had always wished he had a father to take him places. The two of them had a fun day of fishing, and the man had brought some wonderful sandwiches. Fred still made it clear that he didn't want to be part of scouts.

The scoutmaster came now and then and took Fred to do fun things. Fred said that without realizing it, he was finding enjoyment in good, positive activities. But still, he refused to do anything with scouting. He kept saying he didn't want to be part of a goody-goody organization that was so involved in helping others. He couldn't understand why anyone would care about anyone else. To him, there was only one person to look out for: himself.

Then one day, the scoutmaster asked Fred if he wanted to go goose hunting. Fred was thrilled. They left and camped the night before to prepare for the opening of the season the next day. That evening, as the scoutmaster was preparing his gun, some geese got scared up out of the lake. The scoutmaster could easily have shot them, but he didn't.

Fred said he asked the scoutmaster why he didn't shoot, and the scoutmaster replied that the season didn't open until the next day.

"But no one would have known," Fred said.

"I would have known," the scoutmaster replied. "And I have committed my life to trying to always do the right thing."

Fred said he felt great disgust for that. "That's so stupid," he said. "Good guys always finish last."

The scoutmaster kindly said, "Fred, good guys don't finish last. They simply run a different race."

The scoutmaster then challenged Fred to look at the people around him and see who was happier as they reached their advanced years. "See if people who have tried to do the right thing are happier or if people who have only been in it for themselves, no matter who they hurt, are happier."

That really stuck with Fred, and he did look. First, he often found that those who were in it for themselves ended up dead, in prison, or with broken lives. Not only were they not as happy, but they also often lost much of the life they could have had. But he also looked at older people who had tried to do the right thing, and he found they were indeed happier and more satisfied with life. And the more they seemed to try to do good for others, the happier they appeared to be.

This bothered Fred. There was no logic to it. To be happy, you don't think so much about what you want, but instead, you consider more about the needs of others.

Though it made little sense to him, he could see it in the lives of those he looked at. He decided to try it. He joined scouts but also set about trying to do things to help others. He found that when he joined in service projects and did a good job, he would go home with a longer-lasting, more profound feeling of value in his life than when he did something he enjoyed. That was when he determined to change his life and do more to help others.

*****

When I finished the story, the boys were quiet. "I'm sure that's not the kind of story you expected," I said. "But I know what Fred has told me is true. I find more, I would use the word, 'fulfillment,' when I do good things for others."

"Is that why you are always trying to get us to do service projects?" Tanner asked.

I nodded. "That and the fact that they are a big part of scouting. But helping you lead positive, productive lives is why they are part of scouting. We want you to learn what Fred learned and to be a positive addition to your communities throughout your lives."

The boys were quiet for a brief time, apparently thinking about it. I soon had a big plate of scones.

"Okay," I said. "Time to change the subject. The scones are ready."

The boys dug into the pile of scones, slathering them with honey butter or jelly. Even though I had a big head start, I struggled to keep up. But that evening, everyone went to bed full and satisfied, with a few scones left on the plate.

A few boys had damp sleeping gear, so the extra blankets I had brought were much appreciated. The night ended up being chilly once the sky cleared after the rain.

*****

The next morning, by the time the boys got up, I had a roaring fire with boiling water for hot chocolate. Sam and Seth helped me with breakfast. We went through eleven loaves of bread, dozens of eggs, and multiple pounds of bacon. When breakfast was over, the boys headed off to fish. Rod was good to continue helping the least experienced where needed, but even Sam was finding success on his own.

I soon sent the few that were on cleanup off to fish, and I finished it up. I inventoried our lunch food and packed the rest into Rod's truck so we wouldn't have to load it after the hike. I even found time to catch a couple of fish myself, but they were too small, and I threw them back.

At about ten-thirty, the designated time for our hike, the boys started wandering back. They didn't all get back until eleven, so we were late getting started. There was Trailmix for everyone to eat during the climb. Everyone put it with their water and a raincoat into their packs, and we divided out the bread, peanut butter, and jelly so we could share the load. Soon, we were on our way.

Castle Peak is a fairly rigorous climb up a hillside. It is continuously upward. Some boys started out determined to make it quickly to the top, but soon they were stopping to take breathers like the rest of us. As always, I took up the rear to make sure all made it. Sam and Alex quickly started falling behind, so I had them hand me their packs. They still struggled but did better. The extra packs slowed me more from having to take additional caution to keep my balance on the steep incline than from the added weight.

Rod and most of the boys made it to the top by one o'clock. Sam, Alex, and I climbed the last steps to the peak near one-thirty. The final part was interesting. As Rod had said, it was like the battlement of a castle. The rocks jutted out of the mountain like a fortress, and a person had to find paths between them.

Once we were on the top, we found the others were already enjoying lunch, so we quickly made ourselves some sandwiches, too. Though it wasn't a long climb, we had climbed many feet. Being on top of the continental divide on the border between Idaho

and Montana, we could see for miles in every direction. The vehicles on the I-15 interstate far to the west looked like matchbox cars flowing north and south. We enjoyed pointing out different things we could see while we ate.

At the top of Castle Peak was a pile of rocks people had put there. Each of us found a rock to add to the pile. Then, some of the boys rolled a few rocks off the steeper mountain edges, watching them crash far below. Rod and I did have to strongly remind them not to roll rocks on hillsides where some of the other young men were below.

Though we spent a fair amount of time at the top, it seemed like it was quite soon that we were making the descent. I took Sam's and Alex's packs again. The downward climb, though faster, was much more treacherous. It was much easier for a person to lose their balance, and if they did, they would tumble and roll for a long way across sharp and dangerous rocks.

Eventually, we all were down, and we packed everything into the vehicles and were ready to go. That was when we realized Mort was missing.

"Where the devil is Mort?" I asked Gordy.

Gordy shrugged. "I'm not in charge of Mort."

"True," I said. "But if Mort is in trouble, you're usually with him."

"I know he came off of the mountain," Dallin said. "But when we got down here, I think he headed off to catch just one more fish."

"Did you see which way he went?" I asked.

Dallin nodded. "I will go after him."

We all waited for about five minutes, and Mort showed up.

"I have two things to ask you," I said. "First, did you see Dallin?"

Mort shook his head.

"Second, why did you leave when you were supposed to help pack the vehicles?"

"I didn't think I was needed, and I thought if I hurried, I could catch another fish before we left."

"Let me share something to think about," I said. "There are eighteen of us here waiting for you, not counting Dallin, who went to find you. Every minute extra you make us wait is eighteen extra minutes of wasted time—one for each person. If we wait for you just ten minutes, that is a total of one-hundred and eighty minutes, or three hours', worth of time."

Rod laughed. "Thank you, mister mathematician. I have never thought of that before."

"So now the big question is, since Mort is back, where is Dallin?" I asked.

"When he left to find Mort, he took his fishing pole," Devin said. "He probably decided to throw his line in the stream while he was at it. Do you want me to find him?"

"No," I replied. "This could go on forever. I will find him."

It took me about ten minutes following the stream to find him. When I did, he was fishing. When he saw me, he quickly pulled in his line.

"I haven't found Mort yet," Dallin said.

"That's because he came back to camp not long after you left."

We finally got packed up and made it home. Since we weren't sure when we would get back, the boys had to call their parents from the church to let them know we had returned. Soon, parents started to arrive. Marissa was first.

"Hey, Mom," Sam said, "you wouldn't believe all that we did. I caught four fish. We hiked to the top of Castle Peak. We could see all over the valley. We each put a rock on the monument on the top to show we had been there. It was so fun."

"And no one got hurt?" Marissa said.

Sam shook his head. "No. It was kind of dull that way."

Marissa looked at me. "Dull is good."

I smiled and nodded. In that way, it truly is.

8
Rules and Promises

For our June campout, the boys didn't want to go too far so they would have more time for fishing.

"How about down on the river?" I asked.

The river ran right through our community, and I had talked to one farmer that had property on the river. He had given me permission for the boys to camp there as long as we made sure we left it as good or better than we found it.

"Where would we camp?" Devan asked. "Most of the campsites along the river have too many people."

"That's true," I said. "But Mr. Andrews said we could camp on his place. No one else would be there. And he has a beautiful spot."

The boys voted to do that.

"Now that it's past Memorial Day, summer discipline rules apply, right?" Gordy asked.

"I suppose it does," I replied.

Gordy grinned and nudged Mort. Mort looked at Gordy, and Gordy nodded as if indicating something they both knew and were ready for.

We spent the rest of the scout meeting planning the campout. As the boys headed off to play some basketball, Rod paused. "You do know what Gordy's question was for, don't you?"

"Only too well," I replied.

"Eventually, you will have to show the boys that you can stand up to them," Rod said.

I nodded. "I know. I don't like to use physical strength for discipline."

"It was them that chose the rules," Rod said. "They're growing to respect you as a scoutmaster, but until they know you can stand your ground against them, that respect won't be as strong as it needs to be."

I nodded. "I know you're right. I'll have to be careful how it's done. If I take it too far, they could despise me. But I have one question for you. Why do they always want to challenge me and never have the same issue with you?"

Rod laughed. "You see this beard and long hair? I have it for a reason. In high school, you could whip anyone in the school. I, on the other hand, was small and often the one picked on. When I was able to grow a beard and longer hair, I did it. It gives me what my wife calls a mountain man look. I'm still not any tougher, but most people's first impression is that I am."

Now I laughed. "You seriously think that's the reason?"

"I do," Rod replied. "That and the fact you're the scoutmaster, and I'm the assistant. I have even heard the boys talk about how tough I must be because I look like a mountain man."

"Maybe I need to grow my hair and grow a beard," I said.

"One of us can just look tough, but one of us has to actually back it up," Rod replied. "You need to be the one to back it up."

We then joined the boys for a hard-played game of basketball. My shooting had improved, and I was hitting more of my shots. So was Rod. He and I still took the smallest boys on our team against the older, bigger boys. But now we were winning more often. By the time we headed home, I was sweaty and out of breath.

We had talked about just having the boys meet at the camp area since it was in our community, but some of the boys didn't know where it was. So, we met at the church. Marissa still hugged Sam multiple times, but she was getting better at letting him go. Maybe it was because she was getting used to it, but it might have been because it was summer, and she wasn't as afraid he'd freeze to death.

Every boy came; the first time we had all eighteen. Once we were all there, we prayed for safety and were on our way. It only took about five minutes to get to Mr. Andrew's property. It took longer to slowly drive the boggy, crater-hole road. We needed to drive as far over onto the side of the road as possible to avoid getting stuck in the mud. My van would tip when we went to the edge, and all the boys would hold their breath until we leveled out.

When we pulled into the campsite, Steven exclaimed, "Wow! This is pretty! I didn't even know this was back here."

We immediately set up camp. The boys had learned that was one of my rules. They had to have their tents and sleeping quarters ready before they could go fishing. They had  gotten so they could do it in about fifteen minutes. Soon, they were all off to the river with their fishing poles.

There were lots of poplars and quaking aspen trees. Many of them had died and fallen. Mr. Andrews gave us permission to use any of the dead wood we wanted. "It will help to clean up the place," he said.

Rod started a fire in the fire pit while I set up the propane stoves. Soon Rod was off to join the boys on the river, and I set about frying the steaks we had brought for dinner. I loaded the second grill with baked potatoes wrapped in tinfoil. By the time the food was getting done, the hunger and the aroma of the food were drawing the boys back to camp, even before I called them. Only a few stragglers had to be summoned.

As we gathered around before blessing the food, Gordy did something that surprised me because I thought he had learned his lesson at the last court of honor.

At the court of honor, the boys had all come dressed in their uniforms, one of the few places they had agreed to do that. The mothers traded turns bringing refreshments to these events. Mort's mother was the one who had done so for this court of honor. She is an excellent cook, and she had made cupcakes. She had made lots, but for each scout, Rod, and me, she had made special ones. She decorated each of these cupcakes with sprinkles in the shape of the scout emblem.

The refreshments were for after the meeting, but before it had even started, the boys gathered around the table, hardly able to contain themselves. Gordy was the worst.

At one point, Gordy decided one cupcake was the biggest and had the most sprinkles. He set it on a small plate separate from the others, licked his finger, and stuck it in the middle of the cupcake. He then said, "This one is mine, unless anyone wants to fight me for it."

"That's rude and gross," Mort said. "Who would want it after you stuck your grubby finger in the middle of it?"

At this point, not really thinking, but knowing a lesson should be learned, I licked my finger and stuck it in the middle of the cupcake Gordy claimed. As I did, I said, "Guys, *this* is Gordy's cupcake."

"Hey!" Gordy said, "what do you think you're..."

He didn't even finish before Mort, realizing what I had done, licked his finger and poked it into Gordy's cupcake, saying," Gordy, you can have *this* cupcake."

Devin and Dallin were able to do the same thing before Gordy could snatch the cupcake off the table to protect it. By then, it was mostly smashed all over the plate it was on. He looked at it and said, "Maybe I want a different cupcake."

"No way," Mort said. "My mom only made a special one for each of us, and you contaminated that one."

"You contaminated it, too!" Gordy said.

"But we were just trying to help you make

sure everyone knew it was yours," I replied.

"Yeah, right," Gordy growled.

Because of that incident, I thought Gordy had learned his lesson not to be greedy. But that was apparently not the case. There were nineteen steaks. Since there were twenty of us, I had planned to cut the biggest one in half for Rod and me. We would both still have less than the boys.

But as I reached for the knife to cut the steak, Gordy spit on it.

"I'll take this one," he said, "unless someone else wants it."

I could see Mort's face flush with disgust. But then, he must have remembered the cupcake episode. He leaned over and spit on the steak, too. Then he said, "Nope, Gordy, it looks like it's all yours."

Before Gordy could stop them, Devin, Alex, and Seth helped mark it for him. Trying to protect the steak, Gordy knocked it off the grill onto the ground.

"I think I'll take another one," he said.

"Sorry, Gordy," I replied. "There are only nineteen steaks, and there are twenty of us. I was going to split that one, but now I'll just be going without."

Gordy picked the steak up off the ground and tried to wash it the best he could. While the others started eating their steaks, I reheated Gordy's. When he ate it, I asked him how it tasted.

"Like dirt," he replied.

"I guess that's what greediness tastes like," Rod replied.

Rod offered to share his steak with me. I shook my head. "I have plenty of baked potatoes and scone dough. You eat it. I'll be fine."

As everyone was eating, I started cooking the scones. I would eat a bite of my baked potato in between turning the scones. Soon, everyone was filling up on scones. As we got to the end, the plate emptied slower and slower. That was when we heard the sound of someone chopping on a tree.

I looked around, and only Gordy was missing. I knew what that meant.

"I think Gordy is chopping a green tree again," Sam said.

I nodded. "And if we don't treat his property well, Mr. Andrews won't want us coming back."

Rod and I headed to the chopping sound, and all the boys followed. Sure enough, Gordy was doing just as we expected.

"Gordy, why are you chopping a green tree?" I asked, knowing full well the answer. "Mr. Andrews won't want us here again if we don't take care of his property."

"Oh, dang," Gordy said with a smirk. "I guess you'll just have to punish me."

"It's summer now," Mort said. "That means Tom will have to throw you in the river."

"I'm okay with him trying," Gordy said.

"Don't we have to vote on that?" Jason asked.

"All in favor of Tom throwing Gordy in the river, raise your hand," Mort said.

Mort's hand shot up, and so did Gordy's. All the others did as well, except for Sam's and Jason's. Rod apparently didn't think he was supposed to vote.

Mort looked at Sam and Jason. "Oh, come on, guys. Gordy's voting for it. If he is voting to have himself thrown in the river, you should vote for it, too."

"It just seems strange for him to vote that for himself," Sam said, but he raised his hand.

Jason slowly raised his hand but turned to look at Rod. "Doesn't Rod have to vote?"

"Nah," Gordy said. "Leaders don't count."

"That's okay," Rod said. "I'll vote for it if you want," and he raised his hand.

"I guess it's unanimous," Gordy said. "And you don't have to talk to me privately about it because I want you to try to throw me in the river."

I sighed. "Okay, Gordy."

Gordy got into a wrestling-type stance. "Okay, I'm ready for you."

I stepped up to him. "Are you sure?"

He nodded. "You bet I'm sure."

I quickly dipped down on one knee and picked him up in a fireman's carry. Then, with him wiggling and squirming to get out of my grasp, I walked over and tossed him into the river.

The Snake River comes from melting snow in the mountains, and the temperature is never much above freezing. Gordy quickly surfaced and started gasping from the cold. The other boys laughed.

"I bet you're wide awake now," Dallin said.

Gordy climbed up on the bank and headed to his tent with the boys laughing and following. But just before he got to his tent, he turned to face them. "I'm not done!"

We all gathered around the campfire while Gordy changed. Once he was in dry clothes, he came out of his tent and headed straight to the trees. Soon the sound of chopping could be heard. I sighed as the boys headed off in the sound's direction.

Rod laughed. "Did you think one time would be enough to convince Gordy?"

I shook my head. "No, but I had hoped so."

When Rod and I reached the others, Gordy turned to us. "Oh, my bad. I guess I was chopping on a green tree again. All who think I should be thrown in the river, raise your hand." With that, Gordy swiftly raised his own hand.

The other boys slowly raised theirs. I could see that some of them were having second thoughts about this, even Mort. I wondered if they didn't like me throwing him in, if they had felt this was not what they had considered when they made the rule, or what. I think some of them could see how reluctant I was about this, and perhaps, they considered that as well.

Rod didn't raise his hand. I'm sure he could see that I didn't relish this. Gordy told those who were being slow to hurry and raise their hands, and when all the boys finally had, he turned again to me. "I guess you have to try to throw me in the river again."

I nodded. "If you insist."

With that, Gordy went for me. He dipped down and tried to pick me up as I had done to him. I dropped my weight on him and then moved behind him. I grabbed him around his middle, then picked him up, almost onto my shoulder. With him once more struggling and squirming, I walked over and tossed him into the river.

Everyone had followed us, but this time when Gordy came up sputtering and gasping from the cold, no one laughed or joked about it. I'm not sure they dared. The look on Gordy's face probably told them it wasn't a good idea.

Gordy climbed out of the water and headed for his tent. The rest of us went once more to sit down around the fire. It wasn't long before Gordy came out and headed for the tree.

"Hey, Gordy," David said, "you're not planning to chop on the tree again, are you?"

Gordy didn't even answer. He disappeared into the grove of trees, and soon we could hear the chopping. When I rolled my eyes and let out a sigh, Rod half smiled. "Well, you've got to say one thing for Gordy. He's nothing if he's not determined."

Most of the other boys slowly got up and headed back for round three in the trees. A few paused as if they were debating whether they even wanted to go. But eventually, they got up and joined the others. Rod and I slowly walked after them.

When we got to where Gordy was, he tossed down the hatchet. "Okay, so I've been bad again. I don't think we even have to vote this time."

With that, he rushed at me like he planned to make a football tackle. As he got to me, I grabbed one of his wrists in my hand, and putting my other hand under his chest, I used his own momentum to swing him up over my shoulder. Once more, I took him to the river. Half of the boys didn't even follow but just headed back to the fire. As soon as Gordy's head came up out of the water, the other boys headed back. I feel we had all had enough. I hoped Gordy had, too.

But as soon as Gordy had changed into dry clothes, he grabbed a bucket that was sitting near the cookstoves and headed to the river.

"Hey, Gordy!" Rod yelled after him. Gordy stopped and turned to Rod, so Rod continued. "Before you do what I think you plan to do, can I ask you three questions?" Gordy didn't say anything, so Rod continued. "First, how many pairs of dry clothes do you have? Second, what do you think will happen if you do what I think you plan to do with that bucket? And third, did you know Tom was a state champion wrestler and probably the toughest guy in the whole high school?"

Gordy stared at Rod. The other boys kept glancing at Gordy, then at Rod and me. Gordy was breathing hard. I knew he was angry. But finally, he set the bucket down, walked slowly over to the rest of us, and sat down by the fire.

Even with the warm fire, Gordy was shivering. I could see it, and I could see the others noticed as well. I wanted to help him warm up, but I didn't want to embarrass him further. Then I had an idea.

"Hey, everybody," I said, "I could use some hot chocolate. Anybody else feel like having some?"

All the boys except for Gordy said that sounded good. He said nothing. I put some water on to heat, and as soon as heat bubbles appeared on the top, I announced it was ready. All the boys, except Gordy, came and got some. Once they had, I filled a cup and took it to Gordy.

"Hey, Gordy," I said. "I thought you might like this." He didn't look at me but just looked down at the ground. I patted his shoulder. "Hey, you shouldn't feel bad. You were tougher and stronger than many opponents I have faced." He looked up and showed a bit of softening. Finally, he reached out and took the cup of hot chocolate.

I got myself one, and as I was sitting down, Sam asked, "Tom, why have you never told us stories about your athletic days?"

"I thought I'd mentioned it a little, but I'm not sure how it relates to scouting."

"Tell us one," Sam said.

"Well," I replied, "what would be good?" I thought a moment, then told them a humorous story from my college wrestling days. The boys all laughed, even Gordy, and it started feeling like we were all back together again.

"Tell us another one," Mort said.

"Don't you guys want to do some fishing before it's too dark?" I asked.

"Nah," Alex replied. "We can fish in the morning."

I spent the rest of the evening telling the boys stories from my sports years. Rod even told a story or two about watching me compete. His older brother was my age and had also been on the wrestling team. After Rod told one where he especially went on about how efficiently I had beaten my opponent, I felt embarrassed.

"I'm not sure I was that great," I said.

Rod laughed. "Man, you were like a legend to the rest of us in the high school."

By the time I suggested the boys go to bed so they could get up and fish in the morning, everyone seemed back to normal. The boys chose to play a quick game of kick the can first.

After they left, I turned to Rod. "Rod, do you think I did the right thing throwing Gordy in the river those three times?"

Rod nodded. "All the boys know you didn't want to do it. Even Gordy knows that. But he left you no choice. If you hadn't followed through on the rules they had set, they would have lost respect for you. As it is, I think they respect you more because they know you will do what you said."

"I just want to make sure the respect they have for me is because they know I would do anything to help them," I replied. "I don't want them to be afraid of me or anything."

"I think you are okay on that account," Rod said.

I took comfort in his words, and I hoped he was right.

9

Scout Camp, Swim Checks, and Fireworks

We met at the church at five in the morning on a Monday in July. We were going to scout camp. We planned to leave right away, but it seemed like forever before we could. Part of the delay was because I had to recheck physicals and permission papers. There was a final review of our trip permit and one last check off of the tents, cooking equipment, and other supplies.

It also took Sam some time to break free from his mother's embrace. He had never been away from her for that long. She kept saying, "A whole week?" and he kept reminding her it was only five nights and six days. "I'll be okay," he said.

Rod and I did a spot check of everyone's personal gear, and with a prayer for protection, we were on our way. I had most of the boys in my fifteen-passenger van. The rest of the boys were with Rod, Seth's father's, and Mort's father's pickups. Mort's father could only stay long enough to help us get to camp, but Seth's father planned to stay over the first night.

It was about five-thirty when we turned from the parking lot onto the main road. From our angle below the Tetons, we could barely see the sun coming up between the saddle of the two highest peaks. It was a beautiful morning with the dew sparkling silver on the blades of grain in the wheat fields as we traveled.

I led the way in my van, with the three large pickups following behind. It took about an hour to drive to the scout camp. The closer we got, the more the chatter in my van increased, and the excitement did as well.

When I became Scoutmaster, I promised the boys I would work with them on any good thing that they wanted to do. They soon learned, however, that there were things I wasn't fond of. Swimming was one of them.

When I had to complete the scoutmaster swim certification, I thought I was going to drown, and so did the boys. That was why Gordy started teasing me about passing the swim check even before we arrived at scout camp.

"Are you even going to try?" he asked me as we neared the camp.

"I'm not only going to try," I replied, "I'm going to do it."

"We only have one week up here," Gordy said. "Don't you need something like six months just to get in shape?"

"Ha, ha," I replied. "Maybe I will pass mine off before you do yours."

I knew Gordy disliked swimming more than any other boy in our troop, so it seemed crazy that he was the one teasing me.

"Actually, I don't even plan to do my swim check," Gordy said.

"But I thought you wanted to work on the canoeing merit badge," I replied. "You have to pass your swim check before you can do anything else on the lake."

"I'm paying Seth to do my swim check for me," he said.

"No one else is going to do your swim for you," I replied. "First, it isn't honest, and second, you must prove that you can save yourself if something happens."

I started trying to speak to Seth about it, but the boys reminded me he was in the pickup his dad was driving. "Well, when we get to camp," I told them, "remind me to talk to him."

We finally reached the gate and were met by a couple of staff members who welcomed us. I told them which campsite we were in, and they directed us to the appropriate parking lot.

Our campsite was Brave Eagle. The boys had looked at the map and chosen it because it was the farthest away from the center of the camp, and they wanted to be as far away from everyone else as possible. They preferred solitude. But reserving the campsite farthest away from everything also meant we had the farthest distance to haul our gear.

We pulled to a stop at scout camp not long after six o'clock in the morning. The sun began filling the canyon as we started the arduous task of hauling all our gear to our campsite. We enjoyed the names of the different campsites as we walked by them, especially Two Moons, so named because it had two outhouses. It took us until nearly seven o'clock to get everything moved into the camp.

We would have to set up camp later because it was time for the swim check. I had just finished getting my swimsuit on when I noticed the boys had all gathered in a huddle around Mort and loud oohs and aahs were emanating from the group. I worked my way through and found Mort with a massive cache of extremely explosive items. There were fireworks and firecrackers that I wasn't sure would be legal anywhere outside of the military. However, I knew for sure they weren't permitted at scout camp, especially a scout camp that was on Forest Service land. How the fireworks got past my inspection, I can only guess.

"Mort," I exclaimed, "what do you think you're doing? You know very well that those aren't allowed here. If we are caught with them, they could send us packing."

Mort seemed embarrassed, so I decided not to make too big of a deal about it. "I want you to get rid of them," I told him. "You can send them down with your father or whatever, but you get them out of our campsite, and I don't want to hear another word about them."

Mort promised he would, and I felt I had handled the situation with great finesse. Mort's father, having helped bring the boys and the gear up to camp, would be heading back shortly so he could go to work. I thought it was natural for Mort to send the fireworks back with him.

Mort, with two other boys, disappeared toward the main camp carrying the fireworks. They had their swimsuits and said they would meet us at the lake. The rest of the boys put on swimsuits, and we were on our way. We were all carrying our clothes so we could put them on to warm up after our swim. We were still walking to the lake when Mort and the boys who had gone with him showed up empty-handed. I thought they had made the trip back to the parking lot quickly but assumed they had hurried so they wouldn't miss Mort's father before he left.

To my query, Mort assured me the fireworks were taken care of. I didn't have much time to consider it further because the siren sounded, telling us it was time to meet at the docks. We quickened our pace and were soon there.

I always hated this part of scout camp for a couple of reasons. First, I was not the best swimmer in the world and was always exhausted when I finished the swim check. Second, even though it was early August, the water was cold enough that a person nearly had to break the ice off the top first. If the water wasn't flowing, I'm sure it would have been iced over. As it was, in the early mornings, along the edges of the stream and lake where the water was still, there was a thin layer of ice that didn't disappear until the sun came up. The thought of jumping in stole my breath away even before I took the plunge.

I always felt I had paid my dues doing the swim checks when I was a scout, but scouting always figures if it's good for boys, it's good for men. So, I stood in line for our turn in the water. Our troop lined up together and, at the whistle, we jumped in for the swim.

The minute I jumped off the dock and went below the surface, the freezing water took what air I had in my lungs and wrung it from me in one giant gasp. I clawed my way to the surface, gulping air into my lungs.

"Swim!" the young teenage staff member yelled at us. "Swim! It's the only way to stay warm!"

Stay warm, baloney. A scout is supposed to be honest, and there was honestly no way to stay warm.

We had to swim four times from dock to dock. I was struggling by the time I finished the second lap, and by the time I finished the third, I could sense the end of my life nearing both from freezing to death and from lack of oxygen. Both Gordy and I gave up at about the same time.

"We'll try again later," I said, trying to encourage him.

We set up camp, and after we were rested, I turned to Gordy. "Let's go give that swim check another try."

Gordy groaned. "Why can't I just have Seth do it for me?"

"Because you will feel so much better doing it honestly," I replied.

"Not likely," he growled.

We headed to the lake, and all the other boys followed to cheer us on—or, more likely, to make fun of us. We approached the board containing our swim tags, and I couldn't find mine. I hunted and hunted for it, but it wasn't there. Then one of the boys found it, not just on the swim-check board, but on the swim-expert board.

Just then, Seth's dad walked up, rubbing his hair dry with a towel. "Hey, Tom," he said. "I hope you don't mind, but I wanted to swim, and since I didn't have my physical on file, they wouldn't let me. So, I just told them I was you. They made me pass the swim check first, so you're all set."

Gordy smirked. "Nothing like doing it honestly."

I was embarrassed after my speech, but I still planned to do my own. I went to the young camp leader and told him I wanted to swim with Gordy even though my swim check showed as passed. There were also some from other troops who still needed to finish their swim checks. We all lined up together, and at the whistle, we jumped in for the swim.

Once more, as before, the young teenage staff member yelled, "Swim! Swim! It's the only way to stay warm!"

I wanted to say something, but no words came, so I started swimming. Besides, that was the only way to get the swim check finished. I slowly fell behind the boys, and most had finished by the time I turned into my last lap. By the time I climbed from the water, all my troop was there to give me some good-natured ribbing. Though Gordy and I were still shivering, we were soon dressed back into our regular clothes.

As for the swim check, Rod was another matter altogether. At Gordy's badgering, a staff member suggested Rod try the swim. Rod, who was not fond of water of any sort, especially cold, growled that if he had wanted to swim in water that cold, he would have been born a penguin. Gordy suggested that the entire troop throw Rod in the lake.

"You have a death wish, boy?" Rod replied.

I finished tying my shoes and stood up, still on the dock. I didn't plan to get involved in their badgering of Rod. But Gordy turned and saw me standing there, the water ten feet behind me and three feet on either side. He seemed to feel Rod was not a good target but hated to back down. "Let's throw them both in, guys," he said, "starting with Tom."

With that, Gordy and Devon rushed toward me. I guess they figured I might be an easier target than Rod since I was so near the water. But in this they were sadly mistaken, forgetting it would also put them closer to the water. As Gordy and Devon reached me, I grabbed one in each hand by their shirts and, using their momentum, threw them over my shoulders and right into the lake. The next two guys each grabbed one of my legs at the same time. The next two each grabbed an arm. I swung one around me and off the dock on the opposite side, and then did the same to the other. The next two tried to tackle me, but again, I peeled them off and threw them into the lake. The next five, grabbing me at the same time, maneuvered me closer to the water than I thought they could, and much closer than I wanted to be before I was able to peel each one of them off and throw them in.

With eleven of their fully clothed friends now in the water, the other five stopped a short distance from me. Rod, standing behind them on the main dock, growled at them. Those boys turned and headed for camp at a dead run. I was panting from the exertion of the swim, followed by dealing with the latest challenge. I turned to Rod. "How come you didn't come help me?"

"Don't worry," he grinned, "I was here backing you up all the way. Besides, I think they gained more respect for your ability to take the challenge from all of them."

We fished the other boys out of the water and marched them back to camp to change.

"Well," Rod said as we watched Gordy shivering his way ahead of us. "I suppose they won't try something like that again."

I wish I could say I believed that would be the case, but I wasn't sure it would be.

After everyone was dried off, I set out the map of where the merit badge areas were. After a brief consultation, I herded the older boys off in groups, directing them to their different merit badges, and then I led the younger boys, who were less sure where to go, to theirs. Rod wanted to try his hand at the rifle range, so he led a group in that direction.

After getting everyone to where they were going, I started putting together the work rotation schedule.

The morning went quickly, and soon it was lunchtime. The boys filed back into camp, hungry. I showed them the work schedule and suggested that the four boys who had lunch duty get on their way to pick it up. They felt two of them could do it and argued over which two it would be. They argued for so long that I warned them that the food area would be closed if they didn't hurry. They still dawdled along but finally went. Sure enough, they returned empty-handed. The food building was already locked. The other boys were not happy and wanted some retribution. Instead, I took the four with me and talked the food administrator into letting us have our food.

By the time we arrived back at camp, the other boys had settled on a plan to catch some squirrels to cook up and were whittling spears from sticks. Once they were assured the food had arrived, they forgot their hunting plans and started making sandwiches.

After lunch, I persuaded them to be diligent on their merit badges and get back to work. This did take a slight amount of extortion, telling them that if they weren't busy on merit badges, I would have them busy cleaning camp. But as long as they were working, I said I would handle things there.

A couple of boys challenged me on it and soon found that working on a merit badge was a walk in the park to the detailed cleaning I expected.

When dinner time arrived, some boys who weren't in charge of picking up the food came dragging the baskets into camp. They weren't taking any chances on going hungry and had picked it up on their way back from working on their merit badges.

Then the boys who were in charge of picking up the food also came in carrying baskets into camp. It quickly became apparent that we had taken more than our share. We checked, and some of the baskets had our names on them, but some had another troop's name. I helped the boys carry those back to the food-pickup building so I could explain our mistake.

When we got there, I found the person responsible for the food. He looked at me, and after the earlier problem, he shook his head. "You again?"

After I told him the mistake, he rolled his eyes. "That troop came to get their food, and we told them they had already picked it up. Now we find you guys stole it."

"Not stole it," I said. "Accidentally procured it."

I was able to calm him down by saying we would be happy to deliver it. The troop was in the closest occupied camp to us, called Yellow Tooth, so it wasn't a big deal to take it on our way back.

As we walked along, Seth shook his head. "I don't think the troop in Yellow Tooth knows anything."

"What do you mean?" I asked.

"Oh, I don't know," Seth replied. "It's just everything about them. When I passed there on the way back to camp, they were trying to build a fire. I think the only thing they were going to burn was themselves."

"Maybe I should visit with them," I said.

Yellow Tooth wasn't right next to us. We had two unoccupied camps between that troop and us. As we stepped into their camp, I could see what Seth was talking about. In the fire circle, they had big logs. The scoutmaster and a few boys were down on their knees, attempting to light the big logs on fire with matches. The matches kept burning out long before the logs caught on fire. A couple of the boys lit paper, but it quickly burned up while only singeing the logs.

We walked right up to the group. "Hi," I said. We're from the camp farther up the trail. We accidentally got your food, so we brought it to you."

The scoutmaster stood and, with a bit of a grin, spoke coolly as he looked at my scouts. "Aren't you the group that never wears scout uniforms?"

I smiled and nodded. "That would be us."

I looked around the group gathered there. The scoutmaster and every boy had on a perfectly ironed scout uniform.

The scoutmaster smirked and said, "Don't you think it's strange that you're the only troop not wearing scout uniforms at scout camp?"

"Not really," I replied. "To me, scouting is about skills more than ceremony."

I sent my boys to our camp before turning my attention back to the scoutmaster. I pointed at their pile of singed logs. "Been camping much?"

The smirk disappeared from his face as he shook his head. "No. We live deep in the city, and it's impossible to find any place to camp without driving for hours. That's why the boys have been looking forward to this one."

"Mind if I take a shot at your fire?" I asked.

The scoutmaster shrugged. "Go ahead and try. But be forewarned, I think we must have defective wood. We purchased it on the way here, and I think the seller cheated us."

I asked them if they had a hatchet or an ax, but they didn't. I asked one of the boys to grab me some paper towels. I pulled out my knife and took one of the roughest logs. I whittled off some shavings and long splinters. Once I had a good pile, I put the paper towels in a pile, then piled on the small pieces of wood. I also directed the boys to bring me small branches and pine needles from the surrounding forest. I broke the branches and laid them with the pine needles on top. Soon I had a good pile. Finally, I placed three of their big logs in a triangle against each other over the other wood.

I lit the paper, and almost immediately, the whole pile started to burn. Soon the big logs caught fire, and it wasn't long before a roaring fire was blazing in the fire ring.

"Well, I'll be," the scoutmaster said. "I truly thought something was wrong with our wood and planned to take it back for a refund."

"You've got to start small and build it up," I said. "I suppose we all have our talents. I lived in New York for a while, but I'm not that great at living in a city. My boys and I aren't much at wearing uniforms. But we do a lot with survival skills."

I held out my hand. "The name is Tom."

He smiled a much friendlier smile. "Steven," he replied.

"If you need anything, we're over in Brave Eagle, and I would be happy to help," I said.

Steven nodded. "If I do, I will definitely come find you."

By the time I got back to camp, those in charge of cooking were busy under Rod and Seth's dad's direction. At scout camp, preparing the food was something we helped direct the boys on but refused to do for them. As is often the case, it ended up being some non-recognizable burnt offering that would normally have been less than palatable. But in our famished state from working hard all day, we slicked it up.

Rod had put together a delicious Dutch oven cobbler, and I had brought frozen bread dough to make scones. The scout camp food never was enough for our boys. I knew I could always fill the boys up on scones. I pulled out some honey butter and jelly, then started cooking. I went through six loaves' worth of bread dough before the boys showed any signs of slowing.

Once the boys were all lethargic from overeating, getting them motivated about cleaning camp was hard. But the threat of extra assignments got them moving, and finally, the camp was clean. Our "Scout Friend," the junior staff member who was supposed to make sure we got where we were supposed to be when we were supposed to be there, came to remind us of the campfire and opening ceremonies at Council Rock.

When it was time, we made our way to Council Rock. Council Rock was a hill in the middle of the camp at the highest point of camp. Benches had been set up like a small amphitheater in a semi-circular shape around a stage. At the focus of the amphitheater was a massive rock on which the stage was built and was called "Chief Rock." This was where the ceremonies took place. Near the rock was a giant wire cage about six feet across, filled with wood for the ceremonial fire.

We found an empty bench amongst the other troops. We had, by far, the biggest troop there. But my boys stood out in other ways as well. The other troops marched in, all spiffed up in their uniforms. My farm boys worked hard all summer, and, though they always earned lots of merit badges, they saw scout camp as a vacation from hours of moving pipe and hauling hay. A uniform didn't fit into the equation for them. That was an issue I wasn't willing to fight, partly because it wasn't that important to me.

As the campfire ceremony started, there were lots of yells for scout spirit. This was another thing our troop boys detested. We should have cakewalked the yelling contest, being the biggest troop, but our boys just rolled their eyes if anyone suggested it. And to be honest, it wasn't something I relished either. When it came to the fastest-built fire, a tug of war, stick pulling, or anything taking strength or skill, our boys came out on top. But no matter how much the camp leaders encouraged them, the fancy uniforms and boisterous events didn't go over well.

Finally, as the sun was setting, everyone settled down, and the camp director started talking about rules. He was dressed as an Indian chief with a long, feathered headdress. As he spoke about fire safety, he began with the fact that fireworks and such items were not only banned, but were illegal on the forest-service-owned land on which the scout camp was built. As he spoke, three camp staff members marched in, symbolically dressed as the chiefs of fire. They were carrying burning torches, and they lit the massive campfire in the cage.

The camp director continued to talk about fire safety when, suddenly, a loud pop came from the fire. Everyone's attention turned to it, and then, instantly, the whole hilltop turned into a blaze of fireworks and explosions. Everyone dove for cover as fireworks shot from the fire, whizzed past us, and exploded into trees and rocks. Benches were overturned for protection, with scouts and leaders lying prone on the ground behind them. The gathering turned into what resembled an ambush.

Smoke engulfed the hillside. The brush was on fire. When the chaos from the explosions ceased, I ran for the nearest bush and started stomping the fire that engulfed it. Rod and Seth's father joined me in stomping out fires, and our scouts followed our lead. Soon, the other troops and camp staff were doing the same. Gradually, as the fires were all put out, the smoke started to clear. That was when I saw the camp director.

The camp director seemed traumatized. Apparently, it had happened so fast that he had not had time to consider what was going on, nor had he taken cover. By the time all fires were out, only a small haze hung in the air, and the camp director was totally visible. He was near the cage where the fire was.

Nothing was left of the fire or the cage in which it had been built. The camp director stood right near the pile of ashes and strewn wood. It looked like a Civil War reenactment gone wrong.

The camp director now held a burned clipboard with all the papers wholly burned away. His hairline was much receded from just moments previous, and his clothes and eyebrows were singed.

His headdress, made of fake eagle feathers, was a black mass of burned plastic hanging down his back.

Everyone quietly returned to the benches and set them upright. Everyone sat down, ready to continue. To this point, the camp director had not said a word. But then he unleashed on us a tirade about scouting and responsibility like I've never heard before nor since. The campfire ceremony was canceled, and the camp director angrily sent us all back to our camps, yelling at all of us to ". . . think about this inappropriate behavior!" and "if it ever happens again, everyone will be sent home."

As our group walked silently back to our camp, the boys averted their eyes from me, though I'm not sure a single boy felt the slightest bit repentant. But when we got back to our camp, Mort approached me, head hanging. "Do you want to know where I put the fireworks?"

"No, Mort," I replied, "I don't want to know! I truly do not want to know!"

But in all reality, we both knew I already did.

10

Black Bears and the Last Man off the Mountain

Scout camp was in bear country, and we often warned the boys about proper bear protocol. What was not packed away in the bear boxes was supposed to be hung on a board high up across two trees so the bears couldn't reach it even if they climbed the trees.

The boys were quite cocky when it came to bears. "I'd just kick the bears' fuzzy butt back into the woods," Gordy bragged.

Each boy nodded and added his own words of toughness. After I had listened to this for quite a while, I finally had heard enough. "You know, guys," I said, "I wrestled both in high school and in college, and I learned that one of the biggest mistakes a person can make is underestimating his opponent. You guys are talking about these bears like they're wimpy pillows that you can kick around, and they won't fight back. But they are muscle, teeth, and claws with a bad temperament."

Rod then told them about shooting a deer that ran before finally dropping dead in a canyon. He had followed it and worked his way down to where it had fallen. It took him nearly an hour, and when he got there, a bear had staked claim to the deer. He talked about watching the bear rip its claw across the dear, splitting the carcass in half with a single swipe. He said he decided the bear could have that deer, and Rod went to find another one.

Rod then added another story about a man who had shot at a deer and accidentally hit a grizzly. The grizzly had come after him, and though the man had gotten away, the grizzly tracked him for days until he cornered the man back at the man's cabin. Tearing the door from the cabin, the bear came in. The man was trying to get to his gun, but the bear knew about guns and blocked him from doing so. Just as it was curtains for the man, his friend showed up in time to shoot the grizzly and save him. I think the story was made up and something akin to a ghost story, but I must admit, by the time Rod finished, even the hair on the back of my neck was standing on end.

Of course, the bear Rod had encountered and the one in his story had been grizzlies with nasty attitudes. We were dealing with black bears and brown bears that were more afraid of us than we were of them, but the stories had the desired effect of getting the boys to think of the bears with a little more respect. Unfortunately, the bears around the scout camp had been around people and had lost most of their natural fear of humans. And our camp was the farthest out in the woods. Thus, while we were eating dinner on our second night at scout camp, a bear came right into our camp.

At first, we thought it was the boys trying to scare each other. It was only the day after Rod had told his story, and all day the boys had been jumping out of hiding places at each other and growling. This caused a few of the boys to have to do extra laundry because they ran out of clean underwear.

However, this had gotten old, and no one seemed scared anymore. So, when Devan said he heard some grunting around the back of the cooking shelter, Gordy scoffed. "That's probably just Mort passing gas."

Then we all heard the growling and grunting. "Very funny, Mort," Gordy yelled. "We know it's you."

"What did you say?" Mort called from over in the wood area where he was busy whittling. We all turned and saw him, and each of us quickly counted and saw that everyone was there.

Gordy tried to speak confidently. "If that is scouts from another troop trying to bug us, they are going to get it."

The tremor in Gordy's voice betrayed the actual fear that it was a bear. I picked up a shovel and looked around the back of the shelter. Sure enough, there was a black bear. He was high in the tree and no immediate threat, so I called the boys, and they peeked around. The bear was hanging onto the tree with one paw as he reached out with the other to the packs we had hanging from the pole. The packs seemed barely out of his reach, which was why he was growling and grunting. It was frustrating him.

I had the boys move to a position where we would be a safe distance away and could still watch him should he come down. Rod headed to the main camp to get pepper spray to drive the bear from our camp.

As we continued to watch, the bear finally turned his attention to the string that held the packs. It was slightly closer, and with a flick of his claw, the line split in two, and the packs tumbled to the ground. With a couple of quick hops, the bear was on the ground. He grabbed the nearest pack and shredded it to ribbons in seconds.

"Hey!" Alex shouted. "That's my pack!"

"Well, why don't you go take it from him?" Gordy smirked.

The bear knew we were there, but our presence didn't bother him. He just started munching the candy and jerky he found in Alex's pack. The bear had just finished that food and ripped open Devin's pack when Rod and some camp staff arrived with an arsenal of pepper spray and flashlights.

The bear seemed to know when it was time to retreat and took off before they could get a good shot at him with the spray. Rod and the other men left in pairs to try to get a spray shot at him to keep him from coming back. Our scout friend handed me a bottle of pepper spray so I could join the hunt.

"But what about us?" Gordy asked.

"What about you?" I asked.

"What if the bear comes back?" he replied.

"I thought you were going to kick his furry butt."

"Well, I changed my mind," Gordy said. He looked at all the other boys staring at him and added, "I mean, we're supposed to be nice to the wildlife."

I looked around at the boys, and I could see they were all nervous.

"Why don't we all sit around the campfire?" I said. "I'll stay here and keep the pepper spray close."

The boys liked that idea, so I stayed, even though I felt like I was missing out by not being able to be part of the group chasing off the bear.

As we sat around the campfire, Mort said, "So what should we talk about?"

I could sense that his goal was to change the subject so they could get bears off their minds.

I grinned. "I know. Why don't we tell more bear stories?"

They all looked at me like the dipstick of my sanity level was showing empty.

"Let's not and say we didn't," Mort said.

"I'm not sure I should tell Mom about having bears in our camp," Sam said.

After some time, Rod and the others came back. They never got a shot at spraying the bear, but they felt he would stay away for a while. Once the boys felt things were safe, Tanner got up and went to his tent. He came back carrying a big bag and handed it to me.

"What's this?" I asked.

"Candy," he replied, looking at the ground.

"And just where was this?" I asked.

Again, he wouldn't look at me as he answered. "It was under my pillow."

I sighed. "Tanner, if that bear had decided he wanted your candy, he would have just gone through your head to get it."

Tanner nodded. "I realize that now. That's why I am giving it to you."

A few other boys looked at us, then got up, returned with bags of candy, and handed them to me.

"Guys," I said, "do you think we have these rules just to make your lives miserable?"

They just shrugged and said nothing.

"Okay," I said. "This will be a good lesson for all of you to learn. We have rules that help us survive. That's the whole purpose. Let's remember that."

They all promised they would. And though I was sure it wouldn't be our last episode, I knew it was a good teaching moment.

About then, Steven, the scoutmaster from Yellow Tooth, came over. I stood and shook his hand.

"I heard a bit of commotion over here," Steven said.

I shrugged. "We had a black bear come into our camp and rip up some packs."

Steven looked almost frightened. "And you're all still here? I mean, you're not like going to your cars or the cabins or something?"

"He ran off when we got pepper spray," I said, holding up my bottle of spray.

At the campfire program at Council Rock earlier that evening, every scout in Steven's troop wore top-notch uniforms. My boys, as usual, only wore jeans and t-shirts. When the camp directors yelled, "Who's got spirit!" Steven's troop yelled the loudest and won the spirit stick. My boys sat there quietly, looking disgusted.

"Your boys don't seem to have any scout spirit at all," Steven said.

I smiled. "Oh, my boys have scout spirit. They just don't think yelling has anything to do with scouting. But you wait until the conclave games on Friday. I will put my boys up against any troop in lashing, bridge building, fire starting, or anything regarding real scout skills. That's what Scout spirit is to them."

"But don't you want to win the spirit stick?" Steven asked. "You've got the biggest troop and could win."

I shook my head. "These boys are farm boys that spend their days working hard. When I became their scoutmaster, we compromised on certain rules. I wouldn't make them yell for the spirit stick, and I wouldn't make them wear uniforms except for important ceremonies and when doing anything with flags."

"Whatever you're doing with them must work," Steven said. "When I go around to the different merit badge stations, the top boys on the list are always from your troop. I keep wondering what your camp is like."

"You are welcome to watch," I said. "I don't know what you'll learn."

It was getting late, and we were going on our hike the next day. So, I told the boys they needed to finish cleanup from dinner and any other chores. Most grudgingly got up and started.

"How do you get them to do their part?" Steven asked. "My boys whine about everything."

Just then, Seth came over. "Tom, do I really have to haul water tonight?"

"Of course not," I replied. "I'm on the kitchen cleanup. You can do that, and I'll haul water."

"I'll haul water," he said, rolling his eyes and picking up the water cooler on his way to the nearest spigot.

I turned back to Steven. "I always work with the boys. I willingly join the group doing the job they hate the most. That way, they can't say I expect more of them than I'm willing to give. Besides, I can always offer to trade."

I joined in to do my part, and when everyone finished, the boys wanted to play a game of Old Sow before heading to bed. I was visiting with Steven, and Gordy brought me my stick. "Come on, Tom. We challenge you to be the sow again tonight and see if you can get the puck into the center again."

I quickly explained the rules to Steven. All but one boy could get his stick in a hole on the perimeter of a large circle. An empty hole was in the middle of the circle. Everyone was against each other, and if a boy pulled his stick out of his hole to whack the puck, another boy could steal that hole, leaving the first boy scrambling for safety. Until I came along, the boys had always stolen each other's holes, sending the one without one off to be the sow and get the puck. But I played differently. When I played, I took the puck through all the striking sticks into the hole in the center of the circle. That was the ultimate win. No one had actually won before I played with them.

I left Steven to join the boys. I started bringing in the puck, which was just a block of wood. Soon sticks were flying as each boy tried to knock it out for me to chase. They sent the puck flying two or three times, and the boys laughed as I chased it. But eventually, expertly blocking their sticks and maneuvering the piece of wood, I got it into the center circle and stood on it.

"I win!" I yelled as the boys groaned and demanded a rematch the next night.

When I came back, Steven smiled. "I think I'll go teach my boys to play Old Sow."

I smiled. "Be careful. You probably don't want to try for the win until you get good at it. Just do like most and try to knock the puck out of the circle and steal holes."

As Steven left, Seth asked, "Do you think his troop playing Old Sow is a good thing? They couldn't even start a fire."

I laughed. "I guess we'll see."

After evening prayer, everyone retired to bed. With hiking to Table Mountain the next day, we needed to be up early. Rod and I stayed up for a while longer to make sure the fire was out and no bears came back. When we felt it was safe, we also retired to our tent.

We were up early, and we had the boys up by five thirty. Breakfast was cold cereal and bread so we wouldn't have to light fires or cook anything. Before leaving for the trailhead, I read off the things each boy was to have in his pack. The list included water, lunch, a raincoat, a sweater, and other survival gear. The boys all said yes to each item.

Shortly after six, we were on our way. We loaded into my van and Rod's pickup and drove to the trailhead. The climb we would take to Table Mountain was just below the Tetons. It was a fairly safe hike, but a strenuous climb. We would make our way up thousands of feet. The last part was the worst, with steep inclines that could cause a person to slip and fall. But there were no steep drop-offs, so a person would only slide down shale rock if he fell. He would be scraped up, but he would be okay.

Once we arrived at the trailhead, we made sure everyone used the bathroom one more time if they needed. Then we hoisted our packs to our backs and started the climb. Rod took the lead, and I brought up the rear. The sun was barely coming up above the mountains as we moved upward from the parking lot.

We started that early because these mountains were notorious for afternoon thunderstorms. A person could almost guarantee one would come by around five o'clock. Often it was just rain, but they could include thunder and, sometimes, sleet. The hike was about twelve miles round trip, and we wanted to be down by the time any storms hit.

Right out of the parking lot, the climb out of the big canyon into smaller Chokecherry Canyon was along switchbacks and was very steep. We hadn't gone even a quarter mile before Sam and Alex were huffing hard and begging for a rest.

I knew that if we stopped for long, we would not be off the mountain by the time the storms hit. Also, I could see the other boys, led by Rod, moving quickly ahead and leaving us behind.

"Give me your packs," I told Alex and Sam.

They took them off, and I pulled one onto each shoulder.

"Okay," I said, "let's go."

Without their packs, they kept a better pace. We were still falling farther behind the others in the troop, but the distance was not widening as fast. We found the other boys waiting for us when we reached the last set of switchbacks of the steep climb up to the ridge we would follow for the last couple of miles.

"Hey, thanks for waiting," I said, panting as I set down the three packs.

"We had to," Gordy said. "Some of us are out of water, and Rod said you were carrying the only water pump. He also said this is the last water all the way to the top."

"That makes me feel loved," I said.

I pulled out the water pump, and as fast as I could pump the water out of the stream to purify it, I filled everyone's water containers. Once everyone had all the water they wanted, the boys were ready to move out, and Rod started leading them up the steep hillside.

I was still tired, and Sam and Alex were unhappy about moving on. But the storms would come soon, and I knew it. I urged them on, and the three of us moved out, with me at the end of the line carrying all three packs.

When I hike, I like to stretch out my steps and move at a good pace. But Sam and Alex walked slowly, and I felt like a hobbled racehorse. By the time we finally reached the top of the ridge, I could see the rest of our troop was almost a mile ahead. At least, I assumed it was them. They were small dots moving up the last steep mile incline to the top of Table Mountain. I looked to the west, saw only one small dark cloud among many white ones, and felt we would be okay. However, I also knew that up on the mountain, the weather could change with little notice. And usually, big storms started with one small, black cloud.

I urged Sam and Alex to pick up their pace. They would for a brief time, but then they would slow down to a stroll again.

As we walked, they talked. Sam's mother didn't let Sam out of the house much, so he didn't work like most of the boys and was not in good shape. Listening to them talk, I realized that Alex also did little physical labor but spent a lot of time inside playing video games. Even before they were in scouts together, he and Sam had become friends at school. I learned as they visited that Sam spent a lot of time at Alex's house playing video games. I could just imagine what Sam's mother thought of that. I also wondered if Marissa knew what Mr. Handon was like.

I kept them moving as fast as I could. We still had a long distance to go by the time I was sure the rest of the troop was at the top. We kept going, and finally, we headed into the steep part of the trail, the part moving up the side of the mountain. It was deceptive. Looking at it, the trail appeared to be a steady, but easy, ascent. But climbing it, a person realized it was much steeper than it looked.

We had to stop often for a breather. Even with all three packs, I did not want to rest as often as Sam and Alex. When we were about fifteen yards from the top, Alex stopped and turned to me.

"Can we take our packs now?"

"What?" I questioned. "We are fifteen yards from the top, and you now decide you want to take your packs."

Alex nodded. "We want to be able to tell everyone we carried our packs to the top."

I sighed and handed them the packs. They put them on, and it took another fifteen minutes to cover the last fifteen yards. And

more than once, I pushed on their packs to help propel them up the
mountain.

Finally, as we stepped onto the flat tabletop of the mountain,
a glorious view met us. Between the peaks of the mountain, it was
possible to see into Wyoming. And looking back in the direction we
came, the vista opened up so a person could see across the Teton
Valley.

Gordy was there to meet us.

"It's about time," he said. "Rod said we couldn't leave until
you got here."

We all gathered for a quick picture, and then Rod grabbed
my arm. "Tom," he said, "you need to look to the west."

I turned and looked across the mountains. I immediately
knew what he was concerned about. It was only one o'clock in the
afternoon, but the sky was broiling with dark clouds forming into a
storm. A strong wind was blowing toward us, and that storm would
likely hit us within a couple of hours, maybe less. If we traveled at
the pace Alex and Sam walked, we might not even be down off the
ridge by then, let alone entirely off the mountain.

"Rod," I said, "you take the boys that came here with you
and hike as fast as you can. They're all strong enough that you
should be able to go down the trail on the face of the mountain and

make it down before the storm hits. Take up the rear to make sure every one of them makes it out."

I then handed Rod my keys. "When you get there, use my van since you will need it for the number of boys you will have with you."

"Then you will need the ones to my pickup," he said and handed me his keys.

I then turned to Gordy. "Gordy, you are the strongest hiker of the boys. You lead the group going down the face. Keep to the left trail and keep everyone moving and push hard."

"What about you?" Rod asked.

I looked at Sam and Alex and shrugged. "There is no way those two can make the strenuous hike down the steep face of the mountain. I will have to go back through Chokecherry Canyon. My primary goal will be getting them off this ridge and trying to find some protection before the storm hits. The lighting on this mountain is the deadliest part, and up here, we will be sitting ducks."

I then gathered all the boys, pointed out the storm, and told them the plan. I also told them to hike fast and hard.

"I'm going with you through Chokecherry Canyon," David said.

"You're strong enough to make it down the front trail of the mountain," I said. "And you will be safer there with the others."

"I know," David said. "But Alex is my brother."

I nodded. I had Alex and Sam grab their lunches from their packs. The others had eaten, but we would have to eat as we headed down. We all said a quick prayer together. Then I said, "Let's move."

I put on my pack and picked up the other two, one on each shoulder, and stepped out to lead my group off the mountain.

The first part was so steep that Alex and Sam struggled to make it down, sliding quite a bit. I stayed in front of them this time and caught them more than once. They almost took me down a few times, especially with me balancing the added weight of the extra packs. I was happy when we reached the more level ground of the plateau. By the time we got there, I could see the storm crossing the Teton Valley, where the open wind could blow it faster. I could also see the dot that I knew was Rod disappearing quickly down the other trail. I was sure those boys would beat the storm.

I turned to David. "Okay, David," I said, "now that we are on the plateau, you take the lead and keep us moving."

"Do you want me to take one of the extra packs?" he asked.

"I'll keep them," I said. "I want you to concentrate on one thing and one thing only: getting Sam, Alex, and yourself off of this ridge before the storm hits."

He nodded, and we moved out. David set a good pace, but Alex and Sam couldn't keep it, and David had to slow down. They kept chattering as we walked, and I knew that was slowing them. They didn't seem to understand the danger we were in.

"Less talking and more walking," I said.

Between David and me pushing Sam and Alex to hurry, we kept them moving faster than on the way up. By the time we reached the top of the switchbacks leading down into Chokecherry Canyon, the storm was moving into the mouth of the main canyon about ten miles away. I knew it would hit us in under a half hour.

We had to be down off the switchbacks into the canyon before that. The rain would be dangerous enough, making the trail wet and slick. Though there were no steep drop-offs, a person could still tumble down the mountain and get hurt. But what worried me the most was the lightning and sleet. Most deaths on the mountain were from lightning strikes or hypothermia. We had to hurry. Even after we got into the canyon, we had to find shelter. We had to have some protection from the storm.

We moved down the switchbacks faster than I thought we would. I think the sight of the approaching storm boosted everyone's energy, and Sam and Alex got scared. When we reached the bottom, I looked for shelter. A small outcrop of rock jutting out from the mountain was the best I could see. I directed David to lead us to it.

There was no trail, so we crossed the stream and cut through the brush. We had just reached the outcropping when I felt the first drops of rain coming from the front of the storm.

I dropped the three packs and yelled to be heard above the increasing wind. "Everyone, get your raincoats on!"

David quickly started digging into his pack, but Sam and Alex didn't move. This angered me. Why would they defy me in a situation like this? I tossed each of them their packs so they were right at their feet.

"Alex, Sam, get your raincoats on!"

I started digging into my pack, and once I found my raincoat, I pulled it out and looked up. Sam and Alex hadn't moved. I was about to yell again when it suddenly dawned on me what the problem was.

"You two didn't bring raincoats, did you?"

They looked at each other, then back at me, and shook their heads.

"You both said you had them when we did gear check before leaving camp!"

They said nothing. The drops of rain were coming faster.

"What the devil is in your packs, then!" I yelled.

I reached for Alex's pack, and he grabbed it. I jerked it from him as he tried to stop me, and I unzipped it. It was full of mobile video games.

"Video games?" I yelled. "I have hauled these stupid games up the mountain?"

But I couldn't say anymore. We were in a dangerous situation. If the boys got wet, they would probably get hypothermia. I tossed my raincoat to Alex.

"Get that on," I yelled at him.

I had a garbage bag in my pack that I had brought to put any garbage from lunches or other things we needed it for. I dumped the trash into my pack. I turned it with the bottom up and punched a hole for a head.

"Sam," I yelled so he could hear me above the wind, "let me pull this over you."

He reluctantly obeyed. The bag was greasy from the garbage, but there were more important things to think about now. Once I had it on him with only his head sticking out, I dug into my pack and found a small grocery bag. I tied it over Sam's head and tied the handle ends under his chin like a bonnet. I barely got it in place when the rain hit us with full fury.

"Everyone get under the rock ledge!" I ordered.

I pushed Sam in first, followed by Alex, then David.

"But what about you?" David said. You have nothing to protect you."

"You worry about helping me get you, Sam, and Alex off the mountain," I said. "I'll worry about me."

I grabbed my pack in one hand and put it over my head to deflect what rain I could. With the other hand, I pushed the three boys into a tight group under the overhang and pushed in with them as far as I could. Being on the outer edge, I was barely under it at all.

Suddenly, a lightning bolt cracked, lighting up the sky. I could feel David trembling, though he didn't make a sound. I could hear Sam's and Alex's heavy, fearful breathing, which increased as more lightning struck around us. With the lightning, the rain came in torrents. It was pouring down the hillside, and the water flowed over the rock ledge and rolled right through my clothes. The pack I had over my head deflected some of it, but much of it still penetrated to my skin. It was icy cold, and I felt like I was in a freezing river with water as cold as the lake at the scout camp.

The lightning hit a tree near us, causing it to explode, throwing embers in every direction, but the rain quickly extinguished them. The lightning continued hitting trees and the surrounding hillside. One bolt hit the mountain just above us and sent large chunks of rock bouncing down the mountainside. I was especially grateful that I had put my pack over my head to block what rain I could. The falling pieces of rock pummeled my pack, and I could feel the sting clear through it.

I don't know how long the main storm lasted. It seemed like hours, though it was probably only about a half hour at most. The lightning moved on, but the rain continued. With the lightning gone, I knew that whether or not it was raining, we had to keep going to get out of the canyon before we froze. In addition, the wind was still blowing. It felt like it was driving icy knives through my rain-soaked body, and though I knew the boys were probably mostly dry, I didn't want to risk them getting hypothermia.

I stuffed the two packs full of video games under the ledge and quickly covered them with branches. Sam and Alex complained about me leaving them.

"We might be able to come back and get them another day," I said, "but right now, we have one goal, which is to get safely out of this canyon."

They must have known it was not time to challenge me on this because they quit complaining. David and I kept our packs because they had items like flashlights and food that we might need. By the time we were ready to start, I was shivering almost uncontrollably, and my voice was quivering with cold. I turned to David.

"David, you keep us moving. If I start to falter and fall behind, you forget about me. You just keep Sam and Alex with you and keep them moving toward the mouth of the canyon."

I handed him the keys to Rod's truck. "If you get off the mountain before I do, get the boys in Rod's truck and warm them up."

David looked at me with a worried look but nodded.

We moved out, and David kept a good pace. Alex and Sam moved at a faster pace than they previously had. I knew if they kept it up, they would stay warm enough to be okay. I was more concerned about what I would do. I knew at that point that I still had all my reasoning capacity, but I also knew that if I started to suffer from hypothermia, my judgment would falter.

Much of the hike out of that canyon was a blur. I must have fallen at some point because David was suddenly trying to help me.

All I could think to do was to tell him to leave me and keep going. He reluctantly did as I told him.

I kept following, but the boys were moving farther ahead of me. My energy was being exhausted as my body shivered, fighting to stay warm. But then the shivering quit. I started to feel warm and comfortable. I had trained heavily for this type of situation. I remembered a similar episode in my wilderness survival training when some other boys got into trouble. Even so, I had to fight to remember my training as my mind told me I was in deep trouble, even as my body told me I was comfortable and should sit down and rest.

Somehow, because of my training and with my thoughts continually telling me I needed to make sure the boys got off the mountain, I was able to keep myself moving. Sometimes I would stumble, sometimes I would fall, but somehow, I always kept moving, even if it was slowly. The trail seemed to go on forever, and in the rain, it often looked like it was just a dream from which I could not shake myself awake. I lost sight of the boys, but I knew they were ahead of me, and that was important. I had to make sure they were ahead of me. And though I kept wanting to stop and rest, I felt driven, driven to make sure the boys were safely off the mountain.

But soon, my mind began to ask questions. Safe from what? I couldn't remember, but I knew they needed to be off the mountain, though I couldn't remember why. I kept going onward, one step at a time, slower and slower, not knowing why I was going or where, but knowing I needed to keep going and follow the trail. Then I fell and struggled to get up.

"Why do you want to get up?" my mind asked.

I tried to remember why I wanted to get up, but I couldn't. Maybe I didn't really need to. Perhaps it was just a dream. But once more, something inside me said I had to get up. I tried to stand, but fell again. I tried to rise a third time, only to fall, exhausted, to the ground.

Suddenly, Rod was there. He threw a raincoat around me and grabbed my arm.

"Come on, Buddy," he said. "You're less than a quarter mile from the parking lot. You're freezing to death, and we've got to get you down."

He grabbed my pack and pulled me quickly along, and when I stumbled, he would catch me. Almost immediately, we were heading down the switchbacks to the parking lot. And then we were there.

David, Sam, and Alex were sitting in Rod's idling pickup. Rod had them climb into the back seat and put me in the front by the heaters. He handed me a cup of warm water.

"Here, drink this," he said. "You need to warm up from the inside out as much as possible."

As soon as I drank it, the heat from inside of me and the warm air blowing from the heaters started to warm me. It felt like knives were cutting across my skin. The pain was excruciating, and I began gasping. After a brief time, I started to shiver again, and as I did, my mind began to clear.

"We should probably get you to a hospital," Rod said.

I shook my head. "I'll be okay. Let's just get back to camp and get all of us into some dry clothes."

I turned to the boys. "How are you guys all doing?"

"Fine," they all answered in unison.

We got back to camp, and we changed into dry clothes. I wrapped in a blanket in my tent, and Rod brought me some hot chocolate. He then told me the part of the story I didn't know.

He had gotten his group back to my van just before the rain hit, and he had taken them to camp. He was concerned about us being caught in the rain and lightning, so he quickly heated some water. Gordy's dad had come up to join us for the evening and had brought lots of chicken, so Rod had asked him to stay with the boys and feed them. He then drove back to the parking lot at the trailhead.

He had debated what he should do when David, Alex, and Sam came stumbling out of the woods. David explained what had happened, so Rod got them in his truck and got it warming.

"Then I headed into the woods to find you," Rod said. "David said he was sure you were freezing to death, but he hadn't waited for you because you had made him promise to keep Sam and Alex moving."

"Did they tell you about the backpacks full of video games instead of survival items?" I asked.

Rod nodded. "Sam and Alex know their lying and disobedience could have cost you your life. They were almost in tears when they reached the parking lot, thinking you might not make it because you gave up your raincoat to save them."

"Actually, Sam had the privilege of wearing a greasy garbage bag," I said.

"I know," Rod replied. "I could smell him. But it serves him right."

"I think maybe we should have one of our troop meetings and talk about following rules and preparedness," I said.

"I would be a little careful," Rod replied. "Sam and Alex already learned a tough lesson. And I know that when someone talks to me about something I have already learned, it cheapens it. I would suggest you let their conscience be their teacher."

I nodded. "Sounds like good counsel."

We moved out by the fire. When I did, everyone went quiet. Rod made sure that David, Sam, and Alex got some of the chicken that Gordy's dad had brought and some other food, too. Rod also got me some dinner, though in my condition, it was hard to do anything but drink the hot chocolate.

The rain had quit, and after a while, I stopped shivering. We sat there for some time, no one saying anything. Everyone had heard what had happened. Sam and Alex wouldn't even look at me.

Finally, I said, "Wasn't that a wonderful view from up on Table Mountain?"

The boys all nodded, and soon they were talking of the hike, at least the good parts. I never mentioned the storm and the problems we had, and no one else did either. And the next day, Rod and David went to get the packs and my van. They hiked in and carried out the two packs full of wet and mostly ruined video games. It was a lesson I hoped the boys would remember forever without me needing to say more.

11

Squirrels, Canoe Races, and Bears

Later that evening, after returning from our hike, we went to Council Rock for the program. As we sat there, Seth elbowed me and pointed. I looked to where he indicated, and there was Steven. He, along with many of his scouts, were covered with bruises.

"I think you forgot to tell him the rule about the end of the stick having to stay below the knee while playing," Seth said.

After a good night of sleep, everyone in our troop seemed mostly back to normal. We were all still sore, but the boys were back to earning merit badges. I did some archery and rifle shooting. I even did some black powder shooting, something the boys weren't allowed to do.

I went back around ten to take a short nap and check on some food items. After I got up, Gordy stormed out of his tent and marched over to where I was looking for ingredients for a Dutch oven cobbler. "I knew it!" he hollered. "I thought it was happening, and now I know for sure!"

"What?" I asked.

"There is a thief here at scout camp," he replied. "I thought I had things disappearing, so I set a trap."

"Oh, really?" I said. "What did you catch?"

"I didn't catch nothin' yet, but I'm going to," he replied. "And when I do, somebody is going to find themselves thrown into the icy creek."

"If you didn't catch anyone, then how do you know somebody is stealing stuff?" I asked.

"I counted every one of my Oreo cookies before I headed off to work on my merit badge," he replied, "and I had twenty-two of them. When I came back, there were only twenty-one."

I felt relieved that the total loss was only one Oreo cookie. I had envisioned things to be much worse. "Isn't Mort the one sharing the tent with you?" I asked. "How do you know it wasn't him?"

"Because he was with me at the merit badge station the whole time," Gordy said, eying me suspiciously. "But you were here in camp."

"I was," I admitted. "But I can promise you that I didn't steal your cookie. I did some shooting activities. Then, because I was up half the night chasing another bear out of our camp, I did a little cleanup and took a nap. And I never heard anything."

"How could you if you were asleep?"

"Good question," I replied. "However, I think sleeping bags are quite misnamed. I can hardly sleep in one."

"Well, I'm going to catch whoever it is," Gordy said.

"Are you sure you didn't just miscount the cookies?" I asked.

"Yes, I am sure," Gordy replied. "And besides, the package was turned. I laid it out square with my wallet at one corner and my iPod at the other so I could tell if it was moved, and when I came back, it was twisted at an angle to them."

"Let me get this straight," I said. "You laid out your iPod and your wallet to mark the orientation of the cookie package so you could determine for sure if someone was stealing a ten-cent cookie?"

Gordy nodded enthusiastically. "Pretty smart, huh?"

It was hard, but I held back my smile. "Absolutely genius," I replied.

"And it's not just cookies," Gordy said. "I'm sure I've been losing some of my candy, too. It happens every time I go off to work on merit badges. I'm planning on setting a trap for that as well."

"What do you plan to do?" I asked.

"I don't know," he replied. "Do you have any suggestions?"

"Maybe you could turn the volume up on your iPod, and then maybe he'll turn it on and listen to it when he's eating the candy, and we'll know he's there.

"Ha, ha. Real funny," Gordy said. "Thousands of

comedians out of work, and I get stuck with you."

I laughed. "Well, maybe instead, you could get some red paint used for the leatherworking merit badge and put that on the outside of the candy wrappers."

Gordy became excited at the prospect. "Do you think that will work?"

"Sure," I said. "There is nothing like catching a thief red-handed."

Gordy hurried to the trading post and returned with some red paint. He painted some candy wrappers and then headed back to work on merit badges.

I was around camp the rest of the morning and saw nothing unusual, but when everyone returned for lunch, Gordy's painted candies were missing. He demanded everyone show him their hands, but the only person with any paint on them was himself from his sloppy paint job. He couldn't try this technique again since everyone now knew what he had done. But it didn't matter to him because, in his mind, everyone was guilty, and he wasn't quiet about saying so.

"Okay, Gordy," I said, "calm down, and let's try to analyze this."

"That's stupid," he replied. "Just because you're a math professor doesn't mean you can solve something like this by logic."

"No," I said, "but sometimes the answers differ from what a person may think. And often they are right in front of a person's face."

"And if it is Gordy's face," Devin said, "then it could be a real ugly answer."

"Ha, ha," Gordy replied. "Thousands of comedians out of work, and I get stuck with you."

"Let's consider some things," I said. "Gordy, did you zip your tent shut when you left?"

"Of course."

"Was it still shut when you came back?"

"Almost," he replied. "The zipper was up about four or five

inches."

"Was it the same way last time when you lost the Oreo?"

"Yes."

"If a thief wanted to remain unsuspected," I said, "I'm sure he would have tried to leave things exactly the same."

"So why only leave it up four to five inches?" Tanner asked.

I thought about it for a minute as the entire troop stared at me, acting like I was going to get a revelation or something. And then, suddenly, I did get one. I smiled as the answer began to come to me. "Maybe it was up only four or five inches because that was all the thief needed," I said.

"That's stupid," Gordy said. "Obviously, he couldn't crawl in that hole. And I put the candy at the far back of the tent so he couldn't reach his arm in and grab it."

I smiled, and that seemed to build the suspense and curiosity for everyone. "Gordy, were there any other signs or anything?" I asked.

"Well, the thief dripped a little paint in the tent," Gordy replied.

Everyone followed as I went to look at the evidence. Upon inspection, I shook my head. "That's not dripped paint."

"What is it?" Mort asked.

Instead of answering, I scanned the trees. The boys looked up, trying to see what I was looking for. Finally, I saw it. I smiled as I answered them. "It wasn't dripped paint; it was footprints."

"Footprints?" Gordy questioned.

I had seen a squirrel often watching us. But now its paws and whole underbelly were red. I pointed at it. "There's your thief."

Gordy looked up and saw the red paint on the squirrel. He walked over to the tree it was in, and sure enough, the ground was littered with candy wrappers. He shook his fist at it. "You dirty little thief!"

The squirrel shook his fist back and shouted, "Chi, chi, chi!"

"You little beggar!" Gordy yelled. He picked up a stick and threw it up at the squirrel. The stick came right back and hit Gordy on his foot. He started jumping around and hollering.

"Squirrel 10, Gordy 0," Devin said.

And thus, we solved the case of the scout camp bandit. But that was only to be the beginning. The boys started trying to devise all sorts of ways they could get the squirrel. When we finished lunch, it was all I could do to get them to leave this newfound project and go back to the merit badges.

As everyone was about to leave for the afternoon activities, Gordy and Mort had a challenge.

"Hey, anyone want to challenge us on a canoe race?" Mort asked.

"I'll take you on," I said.

"Who will be your partner?" Gordy asked. I looked around the camp. Sam had been really quiet since what had happened on the mountain. I thought it might be good to choose him to help him feel better.

"Hey, Sam," I said. "How about you?"

Sam looked a little surprised that I had chosen him. But he nodded and smiled. We headed down to the dock with all the others following us. We signed out for the canoes.

"Well, this should be an easy win for us," Gordy said. He pointed to himself and Mort. "The strength and brains of the troop." He then pointed to Sam and me and said, "And the weak and the old and fat." He then laughed. "We'll try to go easy on you."

"Okay," I said. "I guess that means we get to choose our race route?"

"Sure thing, Old Fat One," Gordy said.

"So here is what we'll do," I said. "We'll paddle down toward the rocks of the levy where the water flows out of the lake. We'll go around the buoy and then back to the dock."

"Piece of cake," Gordy said.

As we got our life jackets on, I pulled Sam aside. "Sam, I'll take the back and steer us. You just do as I direct you. Gordy and Mort are strong and the best paddlers, but there's more to guiding a canoe than strength."

Sam nodded, and we finished buckling our life jackets. We were another couple of minutes while Mort and Gordy argued over who got to be in the back of the canoe. Finally, we all climbed in our canoes. We lined the canoes up even, Rod gave the signal, and we were off.

Gordy and Mort soon pulled to a bit of lead and started yelling back at us to mock us. We were only about a canoe's length behind them when they reached the buoy. But precisely what I expected to happen did happen. They were rowing with such strength and speed that they shot well beyond the buoy. That took them into the pull of the stream toward the outflow of the lake.

As Sam and I approached the buoy, I directed him to slow his paddling. I brought our canoe almost to a stop, then directed him to row on the opposite side of from the buoy. Then, with solid, even strokes, I guided us around the buoy, and we headed back.

"Okay, Sam," I said. "Paddle with all of your strength."

We started moving at a good, even clip back toward the dock. By the time Gordy and Mort had pulled themselves out of the pull of the water flowing from the lake, Sam and I were nearly back to the dock. By the time they returned to the buoy and started to move past it, Sam and I were pulling up to the dock. It was another couple of minutes after we had stopped before they pulled up beside us.

All the others were laughing.

"It looks like weak, and old and fat beats the big heads," Dallin said.

"Oh, shut up!" Gordy said. He then turned to me. "Do you want to try that again?"

I looked at Sam, and he nodded. Mort insisted that Gordy let him have the back, so they switched positions. We moved our canoes next to each other and, at Rod's signal, we were off again. The same thing played out. Though Mort and Gordy didn't go as far around the buoy, they still went far enough that the stream was dragging on them. That gave us time to get around the buoy and get a head start back. We reached the dock at about the same time, and everyone declared it a tie.

"Tie, nothing," Gordy said. "We won."

"If anything, you lost," Rod said.

When we climbed out of the canoes, I turned to Mort and Gordy as the troop gathered around. "Did you two learn anything from that experience?"

"Yes," Mort said. "I learned that Gordy is worthless at paddling a canoe."

"Me?" Gordy said. "Who was guiding us that time? I would have been better to have gone myself."

"The point is," I said, "there is more to paddling a canoe than just strength. You two could get up fast speed, but you fought against each other as you tried to make the turn. You both were trying to direct it. The reason Sam and I did so well was because he followed my directions. There is an old Indian saying. 'Too many chiefs tip canoe over.'"

"We'll remember that, Chief," Dallin said with a grin.

"Is that really an old Indian saying?" Seth asked.

I shrugged. "If it isn't, it ought to be."

As many of the scouts headed to different merit badge stations, I stayed at the lake for much of the afternoon, teaching the inexperienced boys how to steer a canoe. I started with Sam, putting him in the back with me in the front. Alex was next. I figured he could also use some good time with me. I spent extra time with each of the younger boys. When we finally pulled the canoe up to dock it for the last time that day, I was exhausted. As I stepped onto the dock, my legs wobbled from lack of blood, having been cramped up on the small canoe seat.

Everyone came back to camp for dinner. We were just getting ready to eat when the trouble began. Gordy opened a pack of Rolo candy, ate one, and put the rest on the chair beside him. We were setting the table and getting the food ready when the world's most satanic squirrel snuck up quietly beside Gordy. It was the one with red paint on his paws and stomach. In a flash, the squirrel grabbed the Rolo pack in its mouth and took off down the trail.

"He's got my Rolos!" Gordy yelled, and the entire troop took off after the squirrel. But the squirrel was fast, and even though the boys ran as hard as they could, the distance between them and the squirrel widened. However, when the squirrel reached the tree, the Rolos were too heavy for him to carry up. He made a couple of desperate attempts before the boys, closing in fast, made him drop his stolen goods and retreat to a high branch for safety.

Gordy recovered his candy and shook his fist at the squirrel. "You little thief! You wait until I get hold of you!"

The squirrel, safe on the branch above, shook his fist back and yelled, "Chi! Chi! Chi!" Then he grabbed a little pinecone and tossed it expertly, dinging Gordy on the nose.

"Why, you little fur ball!" Gordy yelled. He picked up a stick and flung it into the tree at the squirrel.

The squirrel retreated higher into the tree and tossed another pinecone at Gordy. This infuriated Gordy more, and he started throwing sticks, rocks, and anything else he could get his hands on. The other scouts joined him, and soon there was a cloud of flying objects. Some of the scouts were not the best aim, and many items sailed beyond the tree and started dropping into the camp.

"Hey!" I yelled. "Throw the other way!"

That was how the long, unending war began. The boys named the squirrel "Psycho," and from then on, there were almost endless attacks from both sides. Psycho felt the camp belonged to him, and he laid claim to anything that came into it. If it was not tied down, locked up, or zipped away, it disappeared into his winter storage. Over the next few days, the boys laid traps, fashioned slingshots, and created crude bows and arrows. But Psycho always seemed to hold the upper hand, especially since the trees were high and the pinecone missiles were plentiful.

I finally got the boys to forget about the squirrel and return to the table for dinner. We were having tomato soup and cheese sandwiches. We had just sat down to eat when a pinecone suddenly hit Sam on the head. Instantly, all my scouts were up from the table and into action. They were ready to make a counterassault. I shook my head.

I tried to eat, but I hadn't even finished my soup, let alone eaten a cheese sandwich, when I heard a noise in the Yellow Tooth camp. There was growling, screaming, and the most tumultuous noise coming from there. Before we could do anything, Steven, the scoutmaster, came running to us.

"There's a bear tearing our camp apart!" Rod and I both pulled out our pepper spray and jumped up to help, but then Steven continued. "The boys dragged an orphan cub into our camp and tied it up."

Both Rod and I stopped and turned to Steven.

"You tied a cub in your camp?" I said.

Steven nodded and spoke in a fearful voice. "The boys found it and said they were sure it was orphaned. They felt sorry for it, brought it back to camp, and tied it there so they could feed it. That must have made some bear mad."

"Not just some bear," I said. "That would be its mother. Sometimes mother bears leave their cubs and go to forage. I'm sure she traced the scent to your camp."

"Even pepper spray might not drive off an angry mother bear," Rod said.

I nodded. "You're right. We could just make things worse. We need to make sure everyone stays out of there until the bear can free her cub." I then turned to the boys in our troop who had come to see what the commotion was. "Mort, David, you two take the south trail to stay away from the Yellow Tooth camp, run back to the lodge, and inform the camp leaders. Gordy, Devin, and Dallin, you follow me through the woods around to the north of the camp to warn anyone coming from that side. I will use pepper spray to defend against the bear there if needed. Rod will drive the bear away if it comes in this direction. The rest of you go down the south trails, warn anyone coming from that direction, and do whatever Rod tells you. Make sure no one goes near that camp!"

I took the three boys I assigned to work with me, and with Steven following close behind, we cut out through the woods to the west to swing wide around camp Yellow Tooth. I sent each of the three boys north along different trails to warn anyone who might come from those directions. I got as close to Steven's camp as I dared and stayed there. From that point, I could hear the bear growling, ripping, and smashing anything she could.

I turned to Steven. "You did get all of your boys out of there, didn't you?"

He nodded. "Everyone ran when the bear came." Then, with his face as white as ash, he asked, "What will you do if she comes at us?"

"We're not standing here to fight her," I said. "If she comes, you run, and I will use the pepper spray to deter her from coming down into the other camps. I don't think she will because she will probably stay close to her cub until she can free him. What was the cub tied with?"

"Just a bunch of rope," Steven replied.

"Hopefully, after she takes out her anger on your camp, she will rip through the rope, take her cub, and leave."

After a while, the smashing stopped, and the growling faded away. I was sure the mother bear and cub were gone, but I wanted to give them plenty of time, so I waited. When the camp directors showed up, I explained the situation.

We cautiously made our way into the camp. The bears were gone, every tent was torn to shreds, and benches and tables were smashed and overturned. Almost nothing was left untouched.

The camp directors were upset. One of them turned to Steven.

"Mr. Dickson, you, your assistant, and the boys in your troop need to meet with us at the lodge right now!"

Steven nodded. "Yes, sir. I will find them, and we will be there." The camp directors left, and Steven turned to me. "Hey, thanks for taking charge. I was at a loss as to what to do."

I shrugged and smiled. "I bear-ly did anything."

Steven only smiled slightly. Maybe it wasn't a good time for a joke.

I gathered my boys from their lookout positions on the trail. We went back to our camp and informed the others. Soon, our entire troop was back in camp.

We reheated our soup and cheese sandwiches. As soon as we sat down to eat, a pinecone landed in my soup. The boys were instantly dashing off to attack. As for me, I simply dug the pinecone out of my bowl and drank my soup, pine gum and all, before another one could land in it.

The squirrel war was getting intense, but I was learning to ignore the barrage of sticks and stones flying all around me, as well as the pinecones raining down from overhead. Compared to the rest of the chaotic evening, it was actually a peaceful moment. At least as peaceful as it sometimes gets for a scoutmaster.

12
Conclave Games

When Steven's troop's meeting with the camp directors was over, he came to visit. Our troop had finally finished eating, hours late after the chaos of the evening.

"How did it go?" I asked.

Steven shrugged. "They asked us to leave because they said we endangered all the troops here. It's probably for the best, anyway. The bear tore apart everything we have, so there are no tents or sleeping bags."

"That seems kind of harsh to ask you to leave on the first offense," I said. "No matter how bad it is, it seems only fair to give a second chance."

"This was actually our second warning," Steven replied.

"Really? What was the first?"

"Two of my scouts got in a fight about who had to do what chores," Steven said.

"That's not unusual," I replied.

Steven nodded. "That's true, but this one escalated out of control. Eventually, one punched the other. The one that got punched fell, and when he did, he landed by the spirit stick we had won that was standing prominently in our camp. He jerked it out of the ground and swung it hard. He broke the spirit stick and fractured the other boy's leg."

"Whoa! That is bad."

Steven seemed to grimace as he continued. "Both boys ended up in the hospital. One with a dislocated jaw from getting punched, and the other with the fractured leg. If you think the camp leaders weren't happy, you should have seen the parents."

"I didn't hear about any of that," I said.

"The camp directors, my assistant, and I tried not to make a big deal about it," Steven said. "I think the camp directors were especially embarrassed that the spirit stick was used as a weapon. Did you notice that there was a new one last night at the fire at Counsel Rock?"

I shook my head. "Frankly, since my boys aren't interested in it, I don't even pay attention to what it looks like."

"Well," Steven said, "I should go help my boys clean up the camp and prepare to leave. I just wanted to thank you, your assistant, and your boys for the help you've given us."

"I'll come help you," I said.

As we walked along, I could tell Steven was discouraged. When we got to their camp, I joined in the cleanup. It was a big job. Many of my young men voluntarily came to help, as did others. As we worked, Steven expressed his love for scouting and how he had looked forward to being a scoutmaster.

"But I guess I'm just not cut out for it," he said.

"I think you're wrong," I replied. "You have the two main things it takes. You love the boys, you're willing to learn, and you know you're not perfect. Okay, so that's three. But the main point is, with your willingness to learn, you will be a great scoutmaster."

He looked up and had a look of hope on his face. "Do you really think so?"

I nodded. "I definitely do. Scouting is about trying and failing and trying again. Anyone who thinks he is going to have a perfect troop and perfect boys must have robots in his troop. But boys who make their own decisions are bound to do some stupid things. It's impossible to eliminate all disasters. Your job is simply to mitigate the stupid things they do as much as possible and help them learn and grow." Then I added with a smile, "In some cases, it is simply an accomplishment to make sure they survive their stupid decisions."

I told him about some of our disasters, including the challenge on the hike.

He shook his head and smiled. "I am glad to hear that. I was beginning to think your troop was perfect in everything except trying to get the spirit stick." He then paused a moment and asked, "Was it your boys that put the fireworks into the fire the first night?"

"Why do you ask?"

He smiled. "I don't mean to suggest anything. I just heard other scout leaders say they thought it was."

"Well, I'm pleading the fifth on that one," I said.

He laughed. "It's just good to know your boys are normal."

"Believe me, there are plenty of challenges with them," I said. "They are probably just different challenges than the ones you face."

He looked at me briefly, then spoke with new resolve. "Would it be okay if I came back tomorrow and watched your boys compete in the conclave games? If I'm going to learn how to be a better scoutmaster, I should start immediately."

"We'd love to have you join us," I said.

We continued to work to clean up their camp. Very little was worth salvaging, and it was almost dark when the last garbage bag was thrown into the dumpster. Steven and his troop loaded into their waiting cars. They planned to drive about a hundred miles and then get hotel rooms. Some parents were going to meet them there the following morning to help transport the boys on home. Steven planned to turn around and come back to camp at that point.

The next day, our boys finished up their merit badges. In the evening, we had the Conclave Games. I'm not sure why the camp leaders called them the Conclave Games, but the games were a test of scout skills. Friday evening was set aside for the competition. There was fire building, bridge building, knot tying, first aid, and many other events.

That evening, Steven showed up just as our troop was finishing dinner. We were almost done when Psycho the squirrel threw some pinecones at our table. One landed in the spaghetti saucepan. Immediately, the boys were up and into battle formation. Rocks, sticks, rubber bands, and any other weapon that could be formed were employed.

Trying to ignore the chaos, I offered Steven some food, and he settled on a plate of Dutch oven cobbler. A rock shot from a scout-made wrist rocket landed on the table as I handed Steven his plate.

I yelled to the boys. "Hey, guys. I told you to aim into the woods, not into camp."

I explained about our squirrel problem, and Steven grinned.

The boys forgot about the squirrel long enough to eat some cobbler before we needed to head to the Conclave Games. When it was time to leave, I gathered the boys around.

"We have a big troop and have been allowed to form two teams."

I then assigned the teams with a team leader and members according to abilities. I chose the best two fire builders and put one on each team. I did the same with the bridge-building and the other events. I tried to keep the teams as equal as possible. I told them the boy I assigned for each event was in charge of that event, and the others were to help him and follow his direction. Rod went with one group, and I went with the other. Steven came with me. It was fun to watch my boys excel at most of the events.

As we finished each event, sometimes we were told we had the best time and score, and sometimes we would find out our troop's other team had beaten us. But either way, the boys from our troop won almost every event, usually taking both first and second.

Steven expressed his amazement. "Your boys are incredible. How did they get so good?"

"It's important to know your weaknesses and strengths," I replied. "I teach them where I am strong. I have Rod teach where he has more expertise. And I'm not afraid to ask someone else if needed."

"How do you get them to behave so well?" Steven asked.

"You remember how I told you my boys set their own rules under my direction? That's critical. It's hard for them to complain if they had a hand in setting the rules."

Just then, Gordy came running up. "Tom, we need you."

The emotion in his voice reminded me of when one of my scouts cut himself with a knife when whittling. I could only envision something similar. I ran after him and soon found myself at a wrestling challenge. There was a large mat. A large, muscular boy from the camp staff stood there with a big grin.

"I've beaten everyone who has challenged me all summer," he bragged. "Boys and leaders. In fact, I haven't had anyone even throw me once."

Gordy pointed at the muscular boy. "Tom, you need to kick this guy's butt."

I turned to Gordy. "I don't think this is a good idea."

"Why?" Gordy asked.

"Because," I replied, "kicking someone's butt is not part of the scout motto."

"Well, maybe it ought to be," Gordy said.

The muscular boy smirked. "It's worth team points on the Conclave Games. But we all understand if you're afraid. After all, you're old and out of shape."

I handed Gordy my water bottle. "Come to think of it, I believe we could use more team points."

It was three falls out of five. The muscular boy and I lined up across from each other on the mat. He was grinning like a Cheshire cat. Another camp worker blew the whistle. The instant the whistle sounded, I dipped down and deftly picked the muscular boy in the fireman's carry. The muscular boy's smile had faded by the time I dropped him on his back.

The muscular boy looked like he was almost in shock and spoke vehemently. "I bet you can't do that again. You just caught me by surprise that time."

On the second time, he shot in. I blocked him, pushed his head down, spun behind him, and locked a death grip around his waist until he could hardly breathe. When I put him on the mat, he panted, "I think two is enough."

Gordy started jumping up and down, yelling, "We won! We won!"

"Okay, Gordy," I said. "Remember my saying, 'The only thing worse than a sore loser. . .'"

"Is a bad winner?" Gordy said, finishing the phrase.

I had almost forgotten about Steven during all of this. But at this point, he laughed. "It's obvious there are some hidden talents in all of this. The way you dealt with that wrestling challenge tells me there are things I don't know. How did you get to wrestle like that?"

Gordy answered for me. "Tom was a state champion and college wrestler."

"I'm sure that comes in handy in dealing with your boys," Steven said.

I nodded. "Sometimes more than you know."

He paused a moment, then smiled. "Wait a minute. Was that you on the first day of scout camp that the group of boys tried to throw in the lake?"

"They tried," I replied.

Steven laughed. "That's funny now that I think about it and realize it was you and your boys. I saw you throw most of them in the lake instead, and the rest ran away. A large group of us heard the noise and turned to watch. I wondered about all of that. But thinking of it in retrospect, after knowing you and your boys, it is even more interesting."

The Conclave Games ended, and we all headed to Council Rock for the announcement of the winners. As we gathered for the awards, the other troops yelled to show spirit, and my boys rolled their eyes and were quiet. But when the awards were announced, our troop won both first and second in almost every event. We also had the only points for the entire summer for the wrestling challenge. When the overall winning teams were announced, it was no surprise to anyone that we won both first and second place.

When Rod and I and our boys came back from getting first and second-place team awards, Steven smiled. "I think the main thing I learned this week is that there's a lot more to learn about being a scoutmaster than what comes from a book."

13

Service and Handcuffs

The bishop came to me on Sunday and asked if the scout troop could do some service.

"Sure," I replied. "Some of them are coming up on advancements in scouts and need service hours. What did you have in mind?"

"Do you know that old shed behind Widow Rosting's house?"

I nodded. "I think I know what you're talking about?"

"She asked if somebody could come help her clean it. Most of the stuff was things her husband collected. He's been gone for about ten years, and she decided it is time to get rid of what she says is mostly old junk. I thought it might be good for the scouts to do it. She said if you found anything of value, you could have it. I thought there might be some things in there the troop could use."

The job isn't finished until the paperwork is done.

I agreed that would be a good idea and told him I would talk to the boys.

After starting our scout meeting on Tuesday, I first mentioned that they needed to get in the last of their paperwork and merit badge cards so we could get things finalized for the court of honor.

"I hate the paperwork," Tanner said.

"But if you don't get it in," I replied, you don't get your merit badges and advancements." I then went to the scout closet. I pulled out a piece of paper. "Mr. Hanstrom from the scout committee gave me this when we came home from scout camp. This is a reminder."

I posted it on the bulletin board. The boys gathered around to look at it. It was a picture of an outhouse with the words, "The job isn't finished until the paperwork is done." The boys laughed and got the message.

When we finished discussing scout camp and the upcoming court of honor, I mentioned the bishop's request.

"Not another service project," Gordy grumbled. "Last time it took us so long we didn't get to do anything fun."

"This job might be interesting," I replied. "Have you ever gone through an old shed? You never know what fascinating things you might find. This is stuff Mr. Rosting collected through the years, and we get to keep anything we feel is useful. The troop gets first option on items, but if there is something you want that the troop can't use, you may keep it."

That hardly ignited fires of excitement in them, so I tried to build it up more.

"I didn't know Mr. Rosting's myself," I said. "But I heard he did a lot of different things in his life." I then turned to Rod. "Rod, you lived here all your life. Did you know Mr. Rosting?"

Rod nodded. "He was an incredible person and had lots of different jobs. I know that he was a police officer for a while. He was a forest ranger at one point. He was a volunteer fireman. He also ran cattle on his small farm. He probably did other things that I don't even know about."

I can't say the boys were excited about doing service the next week, but the thought of treasure hunting through a shed, and Rod's words, increased their enthusiasm to a mediocre level. "This will be a good thing," I said. "Besides, some of you need service hours for your next scout rank advancement."

The following Sunday, I reminded the boys about the Tuesday activity. "Don't forget the service meeting on Tuesday. We will be helping Old Widow Rosting clean out her shed, so come an hour early and dress in old work clothes."

When we arrived at Widow Rosting's, she smiled. "Thank you for doing this. I can't tell you what's in there. In addition to being an avid collector, my husband worked at a lot of different jobs in his lifetime. If you find anything you would like, you're welcome to keep it."

When we went around the house, the sight of the old shed seemed to intrigue the boys, who chattered excitedly. I led the way to the shed and lifted the hook that latched the door. The door unwillingly squeaked open as I pushed against it. I stepped in, trying to find a light switch, and was engulfed in spider webs. I wrapped up the webbing and pulled it from my face and hair while I continued my search. I eventually found what I was looking for and clicked the switch, dimly lighting the shed with more shadows than light.

Some of the boys held back, reluctant to enter the dusty shed, while others rushed ahead of me, hoping to be the first to find something interesting. Soon the boys were scurrying all over. When a boy would find a treasure, he would bring it to me. If the troop could use it, we set it aside for troop use. If it wasn't something the troop could use and the boy wanted it, he would slip it into his seat in my van or Rod's pickup to take home with him. If junk was found, it was put into the back of Rod's pickup.

Devin brought me an old fireman's ax. It was an ax on one side and a pick on the other. We decided that it could be useful for scouting. Some of the boys brought old cast iron pans that we could add to our scout supplies once they were cleaned.

I took a load of trash out, tossed it into Rod's truck, and turned around to find Gordy and Mort, side by side, grinning at me. "Guess what we found?" Mort said.

"A mummy?" I replied.

They laughed, then Gordy said, "Not quite. But something almost as good. Look at this."

They each held up a wrist, a pair of handcuffs between them. "Aren't they cool?" Mort asked.

I stared at them as they continued to grin, and asked, "You do have a key, don't you?"

Suddenly, their grins disappeared as their predicament dawned on them.

Gordy turned to Mort. "You do have a key, right?"

"Me?" Mort replied. "It was your idea to put them on."

The other boys and Rod gathered around. "Well, well, well," Rod said, looking at Gordy and Mort, "don't you two make the cutest couple holding hands like that?"

"We aren't holding hands!" Gordy said. "Idiot Mort handcuffed us together."

"If I were to allow someone to handcuff themself to me, it would have to be a girl who is a lot better looking than either of you two are," Rod said.

I laughed. "What I want to know is which of your houses you two plan to live at."

"Just shut up and find a key so I can get away from stupidilla before I am infected with stupidness," Mort said.

"I think it might be too late for that," Devin smirked.

I told the boys to spread out and search for a key. We turned the shed upside down but didn't find one. It grew time for the boys to go home, and we still had most of the shed to finish since we had turned our attention to hunting for the key. We decided I should take the other boys home and notify Mort and Gordy's parents that Rod was taking their two sons to the sheriff's office to get them separated.

When I checked later, I learned that the only thing the

Sheriff's office was able to do was cut the chain connecting the handcuffs. Eventually, Rod took the boys to the fire department, and they used equipment for cutting into cars to remove the handcuffs from their wrists.

Since we didn't finish the shed that first week, the following week we planned our meeting to work on it again. I was sure that since Gordy and Mort had handcuffed themselves together the week before, everyone would be more careful with what they found. The scouts had hoped to have a game night and weren't too sure about more service.

"Hey," I said. "It wasn't my fault that Gordy and Mort handcuffed themselves together."

"Cleaning the shed isn't so bad," Devin reminded the others. "There are lots of cool old things in there."

I promised them that if they worked hard, we would make sure we went back in time to play some basketball. We went to work, and the boys soon found more interesting things and enjoyed themselves as we worked our way deeper into the shed.

"What's this?" Dallin asked, holding up a rusty tin box.

"I'm surprised at you," I replied. "Haven't you ever seen an electric fence charger before?"

"Is that what it is?" Dallin asked. "I haven't seen one this old before."

"It's probably not as old as Tom," Gordy said. "That's why he knows what it is."

"It's almost an antique," Devin said.

"Just like Tom," Gordy added.

"I bet it doesn't work anymore," Dallin added.

"Just like Tom," Gordy said.

"Okay, Gordy," I said. "I think they got the picture."

"I suppose you could plug it in and find out if it works," Rod told them, flashing me a grin. I immediately knew he was up to something.

"Great idea," Gordy replied. "Let's find an outlet."

I sidled up near Rod and whispered, "You know this is going

to end badly, don't you?"

He nodded. "Of course. That's why it should be fun."

The boys eventually found an outlet on the outside of the shed. They plugged in the charger and looked at it. "Now what?" Mort asked.

"Touch it and see if it works," Rod said.

"How stupid do you think I am?" Mort asked.

"Do you really want us to answer that after you and Gordy handcuffed yourselves together last week?" Steven asked.

"I'm sure it was just rhetorical," I answered.

"I heard that if a person touches a wet piece of grass to a charger, it will sparkle," Gordy suggested.

Seth grabbed a piece of grass and handed it to Gordy. Gordy spit on it and touched it to the positive node. Nothing happened. Feeling brave, Gordy touched the node. Still nothing.

"I told you it wouldn't work," Devin said. "It's too old."

Rod whispered to me, "You're familiar with these. Do you think it still works?"

"I've felt the jolt of ones older than this," I replied. "The problem is that they are not completing a full circuit. There has to be a wire grounding the negative node."

"Of course," Rod said. He then turned to the boys. "Maybe the problem is that you don't have a long enough line. You know fences are long. Why don't you form a human chain? Gordy will hold on to the charger, and each of you can grab on to the next person in line, and maybe you will eventually feel something."

The boys thought that was a great idea and started lining up. After each additional boy grabbed hold of the one in front of them, Rod asked if they felt anything. The answer always came back negative.

Rod was standing with gloves on, holding the charger in one hand and one end of a wire in his other. His foot was on the other end of the wire. I was sure I knew what he had in mind. Finally, the last boy was connected in the line, and when Rod asked if they felt anything, they all replied, "Nothing yet."

Rod grinned. "See if this helps." He then touched the end of the wire he was holding to the grounding terminal on the charger.

Instantly, there were screams from all the boys as the nonlethal charge gave them a good jolt.

Rod grinned. "Good job, guys. I guess you proved the charger still works after all."

"That's not all we learned," Mort said. "We learned not to trust you."

As the boys returned to cleaning and treasure hunting, I asked, "Do you think they've learned a lesson on this with the handcuffs and the charger?"

Rod laughed. "Not likely. They're scouts. Curiosity will get still get them the next time."

14

Ice Fishing and Winter Camping

With fall came school. David had graduated from high school, so he was off to college. I could tell Alex felt lost without him, but he continued to come to all the campouts in the fall.

We camped every month from September through November, but everyone had conflicts in December, so we weren't able to go camping then.

For the winter campout in January, the boys wanted to go ice fishing on Henry's Lake. Their excitement was contagious as we prepared and talked about proper dress and keeping warm. Rod, who was a much better fisherman than I was, told the boys that the best bait for ice fishing was worms.

"With the cold, there are no bugs for the fish to eat. And with the ice covering the lake, there would be no way for them to get bugs anyway. So, some live food is very tempting to them."

Sam was excited, but I could tell by the look on his face that he was also worried about something. After we finished our scout meeting for the night, and the other boys headed off to play basketball, he hung back. I realized he wanted to talk to me.

"Tom," he said, "I'm concerned that my mom won't let me go if she knows we are going to be fishing out on the ice."

"Why?" I asked.

"She has watched lots of shows where someone falls through the ice and can't get out. That has been one of her biggest fears about living here in the winter. She won't let me or my younger brother or sisters do anything near ice in the winter. When I came back from our camp at Porcupine Creek, and she found out I fell in, that about ended me getting to do scouting. It would have, except for the fact that she was amazed you would go in after me."

"Is there something I can do?" I asked.

"Could you just talk to her and assure her it's safe?"

I nodded. "Sure."

We joined the other boys and Rod in a tough game of basketball. When it was time to head home, I gave some of the boys rides, as I often did. When Sam was the only one left, we drove to his house.

Sam led the way into his house, and when I entered, Marissa cringed. She hadn't known I would be coming in and the place looked lived in. It didn't bother me, but it seemed to bother her that she hadn't known to tidy it up.

"Mom," Sam said, "we have a campout this Friday and Saturday."

"Oh," Marissa said, raising her eyebrows. "Where are you going?"

She turned to me when she said this, and I realized, as Sam seemed to, that she was directing the question to me.

"We are going ice fishing up on Henry's Lake," I said.

"Fishing for ice?" she said in a bewildered tone. "Why would you fish for ice?"

"We don't fish *for* ice," I replied. "We fish through the ice."

"You mean you get right on the ice to fish?" she said, panic sounding in her voice. "What if someone falls through?"

"No one will fall through," I replied. "The ice is so thick that I know of people who have driven pickups on it. In fact, I heard a funny story the other day. A guy drove his pickup out on the ice, and the ice was so thick he couldn't chop a hole through it to fish. So, he lit some dynamite and tossed it onto the ice to blow a hole through. The man's dog thought his owner wanted to play fetch, so the dog went and got the dynamite and started bringing it back. The man saw the dog carrying the lit dynamite back to him, so he started yelling at the dog. The dog didn't know what to do, but he knew the man didn't want the dynamite. So, the dog hid the dynamite under the pickup and came to the man expecting praise."

I started to laugh as I finished. "The dynamite exploded and blew a hole in the ice, and the pickup was sunk in the lake."

I laughed as I finished what I thought was a great story. But I looked at Marissa, and she was staring at me with wide eyes. She definitely was not laughing, and I could tell I was not helping Sam's cause.

"The pickup fell through the ice?" Marissa asked.

"Well, yes, but only after the dynamite blew a hole in the ice."

"Are you going to be driving out on the ice?"

I shook my head. "No. That is a stupid thing to do. I was just telling it as a fun story. We will only be walking on the ice."

"Are you going to blow holes through the ice with dynamite?"

I again shook my head. "That would actually be illegal."

"But if the man with the truck did . . ." Marissa started to say.

"It was just a story," I said, cutting her off before her thoughts could wander too far. We will just walk out on the ice and fish through holes."

"How will you make the holes?" Marissa asked.

"Rod, my assistant, has a machine with an auger that will drill the holes through the ice."

"But what if one of the boys falls through a hole?" she asked

"They won't," I replied. "The holes will be too small for a person to fall through. The hole will only be big enough to put in a fish line and pull a fish through."

"I don't know," she said. "What if the ice doesn't hold the weight of all of you?'

"Marissa, I understand your concern," I replied. "But the ice will hold us. The temperature has been thirty degrees below zero up there, and it is thick. There are stories of pioneers taking ox teams and wagons across frozen rivers, and we don't weigh as much as oxen." I laughed. "Well, at least the boys don't. I might."

Marissa didn't even smile. All my attempts at humor were falling flat with her. But then she got another worried look on her face.

"Thirty degrees below zero?" she said. "How could you

survive?"

"Look, Marissa, you don't need to worry. We've trained the boys well to deal with the cold. We even have a little wood stove that goes in the tent. They will be fine. Sam will be fine. I promise."

She looked into my eyes, and I could sense her fear, yet behind it, I also sensed a strong depth of trust in me. She looked at Sam's hopeful face, and finally, she nodded.

"Sam has a list of things he needs to bring to be prepared," I said. "If he has those, he will be fine. If you are missing anything, give me a call, and I will make sure he has what he needs."

"I do need another fishing pole," Sam said. "I broke mine on the last campout."

"He's been asking me to buy one for him," Marissa said, "but funds have been short.'

"That's not a problem," I replied. "I have extras."

As I drove home, I considered that I should be careful how I joke with Marissa. She didn't seem to find any humor in outdoor activities.

On Thursday after work, I purchased all the food we needed. On the way home, I stopped at a gas station and purchased a bunch of worms to ensure we had plenty of bait. I also got hooks, sinkers, line, and other items I thought might be needed.

While I was there, I renewed my fishing license. The boys who were under fourteen didn't have to have licenses as long as a leader had one. I was sure Rod would have his. As much as he fished, I'm sure his license seldom expired for more than a few days at the first of the year. But I wanted to make sure I had mine as well.

I got the Dutch ovens, grills, propane cook stoves, fishing poles, and other things we would need together and ready to load after work the next day. I had a bag of hand warmers, extra blankets, and sleeping bags just in case they were needed.

Friday after work, I hurried home as fast as I could. I loaded everything into my van and headed to the church. Rod and the boys were already there. It was barely after five, our agreed-upon meeting time, but they talked like it was midnight, and they had been waiting for me for hours.

The boys helped move the food and camping goods to the back of Rod's pickup. We made sure milk and items like that were in coolers, not to keep them cold but to keep them from freezing. The temperature was dropping quickly.

Sam was there when I got there, and Marissa was, too. She always had a tough time sending Sam off and often stayed until the last minute. Sam kept reassuring her he would be fine. One boy I was surprised to see there was Jason. He often missed the winter camps.

"Jason, it's good to see you," I said.

He pulled his fogged-up glasses from his face and looked at me. "Well, I get tired of hearing about all the fun you guys have and not being part of it. I just hope I don't freeze to death."

"If you got all of the items I had on the list for you, you'll be fine," I said.

We were finally packed up and ready to go. After a quick word of prayer, everyone loaded into the two vehicles, and we were on our way. Marissa had to give Sam one last kiss, which embarrassed him.

It took about forty minutes to get to Henry's Lake, so it was nearly dark when we arrived at the campsite. Using flashlights and lanterns, Rod and the boys set up the camp while I cooked dinner. Under Harry's direction, the community had purchased a nice wall tent with a wood stove. It was big enough for all twenty sleeping bags if we all tucked in tightly. Rod and I would be right by the door, farthest from the heat.

For dinner, I cooked hamburgers. I had purchased enough meat, buns, and fixings for four apiece. They went fast, and obviously, some must have eaten more than four because I had to set aside the last one for myself to have any at all. I even had fries to go with them, and those were all gone, too. I always try to have three to four times what an average person will eat. But no matter how much

I brought, the boys always finished it off. When I mentioned that to Rod, he said, "That's because scouts aren't normal people."

As usual, I had scones to make sure everyone had enough. I had brought fifteen loaves worth of bread, and only a few loaves were left when the boys finally said they were full.

"If I eat one more bite, I will need a bloat needle," Dallin groaned.

As everyone was finishing, we gathered around the fire to keep warm.

"Tom, tell us a story," Sam said.

"Yeah," Gordy said. "You tell the best stories."

"What kind of story should I tell?"

"Have you ever run into problems on a campout because of cold or other problems?" Sam asked.

I nodded. "More time than I like to remember."

"Tell us about one," Sam said.

"Okay," I said. "Let me tell you about one when I was about the age of some of you. That fall, our troop decided we wanted to go to scout camp the following summer. In the community I grew up in, our troop hadn't been to scout camp for many years. But our scout committee felt that if we wanted to go, we should work for it. People in the community offered us jobs to earn the money. I would work all day, and by evening when we were supposed to go earn the money, I was exhausted. But I was the patrol leader, and knew I needed to go. But too often, when I would get to the money-earning project, I would be the only one there. But that is a story for another time.

"We did earn enough money and went to scout camp the following summer. It was in late June, before the hay hauling would keep me home. At camp, I signed up for the wilderness survival merit badge. We went through all our training, and then we were to spend two days and a night in the wilderness on our own. We were not allowed to take food, but had to subsist on what we found in the wilderness.

"We were only allowed to take basic stuff, a little bit of extra clothing such as raincoats for emergencies, a flashlight, a knife, a limited bed roll, and flint and steel to make fire. Most of what we had to use to survive had to come from what we found around us.

"We were taken up onto the mountain in a couple of vans and left there with two leaders. The vans then headed back to camp. We were given directions to spread out, trying to distance ourselves from each other at least a hundred yards apart. If we ran into a fellow scout, we were supposed to act like we didn't see them and continue to do everything on our own.

"We were taught that the first rule of survival is proper shelter. When we got to the place where we decided to set up our individual camps, we were to create a shelter. Once I found what I felt looked like a good place for my camp, I started preparing my shelter.

"I found a good solid tree that had blown over. I found lots of thick branches and poles and leaned them against the big tree to make a lean-to. I cut some thin willows and used them like string to lash the branches to the tree as best as I could. I then covered the pole with branches, especially evergreen ones that I found.

"I used my knife to cut long, dry grass and pieces of shrubs. I packed those on top of the branches to shed water; then, I put more branches on to hold the grass and shrubs in place. As I was getting about done, I noticed some ominous-looking clouds rolling towards the mountain, coming from the west. I got some wood in my shelter, so I would have some that was dry and be able to start a fire. Then I quickly looked for food. All I was able to find were some wild strawberries that weren't even close to being ripe. I ate them anyway because I was hungry, and it took away the hunger pains.

"Other than that, I could only find a few old, dried chokecherries from the previous year. I had just picked them when the storm hit, so I put on my raincoat. I was not about to try to eat the chokecherries plain. They are so bitter. So, I hurried inside my shelter and built a little fire at the lean-to entrance so the smoke would go out. I had a small pan we were allowed to have, and I filled it with rainwater and started to heat it on the fire. I put the dried chokecherries in the pan as the water began to boil. It was nasty tasting, but as hungry as I was, it didn't matter.

"I was drinking the bitter water when the storm increased to incredible ferocity. The rain turned to freezing sleet and hail, driving me farther into my shelter. A few drips were coming through the roof, but mostly I stayed dry. I was also able to plug most of them and did so as much as possible. The wind was whipping the fire into the shelter, so I laid out my bed roll and laid down. The air at the bottom of the shelter was less smoky because the smoke was rising.

"With the sleet and hail, the temperature plummeted well below freezing, down around zero degrees, incredibly cold for a summer evening, even for the Idaho mountains. The storm had also darkened the sky, even though the sun was up, so I finally decided I might as well turn in for the night. I decided that if I climbed in my bedroll, I would stay warmer. I had just put on any extra clothes I had for more layers, and climbed into my bedroll, when a flashlight shone in my face.

"It was one of the camp leaders. He said he hated to ask, but they desperately needed my shelter. Two boys had broken all the rules. First, they had not gone out on their own but had stayed together. Then they played Frisby instead of putting their shelters together. When the storm hit, they were unprepared and didn't even have rain gear. The two boys had gotten soaked and were freezing and had hypothermia.

"The camp leaders had tried to use their radio to call back to camp, but the storm was making it impossible. 'You and another boy have the best shelters we've found,' the camp leader said. We want to take your shelters to try to save the lives of the scouts that didn't prepare.'"

"I got dressed and even left them with my bed roll. One of the boys who didn't prepare climbed in my bedroll while the leader warmed some water over my fire to give to the boy to warm him.

"The other boy, whose shelter the leaders had asked for, joined me, and together we built a shelter as quickly as we could with the sleet and hail beating down on us. He started forming sticks together in a teepee shape while I gathered evergreen branches to put over them. The storm made the darkness of the evening like midnight even though the sun was just setting. I tripped and fell more than once, and I know the other boy did as well. We worked as fast as possible using our flashlights to see. The lightning was flashing all around us. I kept thinking that if we didn't freeze to death, we would probably be killed by lightning.

"The shelter we made was not as good as my first one, but eventually, we were able to crawl inside. It was not tall enough to stand in. We could only sit, and there was not enough room to lie down, so we each had to curl in a ball to sleep.

"The storm raged most of the night, but finally, an hour or so before dawn, it quit. The sky cleared, and when it did, the temperature dropped even lower. I had hardly slept all night because I was shivering so much. The same was true for the other boy.

"I don't think I have ever been so happy to see the sun as I was that morning. When the light started to show above the mountain, it filled me with hope and happiness. Everything around us was covered in ice, and despite our desperate state, it was beautiful. It was like a million prisms hanging from trees, bushes, and our little shelter. It was hard to believe it was June, but in the mountains, any weather is possible in any month.

"All night, I wondered if we would make it through the night. But as the sun rose in the sky, it started to warm, and I knew we would be okay."

"What happened to the two boys who had gotten

hypothermia?" Dallin asked.

"They fared okay," I replied. "They were in our warm shelters and had food that the camp leaders had brought for an emergency. The radio didn't work until things dried out around noon. The road had washed out, and they couldn't get the van to us. They were able to bring in a couple of all-terrain-vehicles and get those boys to a van to take them to the hospital. Those two boys stayed there for a day for evaluation. And the leaders told us those two boys would definitely not be earning their emergency preparedness merit badges."

"I would think not," Dexter said.

"What about the rest of you?" Devin asked.

"We had learned about the road washout when search and rescue people came to get the two boys that went to the hospital. It was about a mile or two from where we were on the mountain. One leader went with the boys to the hospital, and the other stayed with us. We got everyone gathered together, and we hiked down to where the washout was to catch rides back to camp in the vans."

"Did you have any food?" Sam asked.

"The storm had created such a mess that finding food was almost impossible. But there were plenty of willows, so I took my knife and skinned the bark off one and sucked on it."

"Is that food?" Justin asked.

"Not really food, but pain reliever. The juice inside the bark of a willow tree is kind of like aspirin and relieves the pain. We've talked about that in some of our survival meetings."

Seth nodded. "I remember."

"Tell us another story," Sam said.

I laughed. "I thought you guys wanted to go fishing in the morning. If I tell you any more stories, you won't be able to get out of bed until noon."

"Yeah," Sam said. "And I want to catch my first fish before the sun is up."

"That might be pushing it a little," Rod replied.

"I'll tell you what," I said. "I will get up, make breakfast, and even do the cleanup. That will leave the rest of you more time for fishing."

"And I'll get up and get holes drilled in the ice for everyone," Rod said.

The boys liked that idea. We had a group prayer; then everyone headed to their beds. I passed around hand warmer packets and had the boys put them in their sleeping bags by their feet. I handed around extra, thick blankets for those who needed them.

The clouds had rolled in. The temperature was about ten degrees below freezing, not too bad for that time of year on the mountain. But as I climbed into my bed, I shivered. I don't think it was as much because it was cold as it was thinking about that night of wilderness survival many years earlier

15

Keeping Worms Warm

The following day, it was chilly. The temperature had dropped more overnight, but it didn't feel like it was below zero. That meant that the sun would warm things up into about the twenties, and it would be a pleasant day.

The first thing I did when I got up was to make a good roaring fire. The water cooler was full of ice, so I chipped out a good chunk of it and filled the Dutch oven. I set it next to the fire to heat it. I also put the water cooler near the fire, but not so near that it would hurt the cooler. I also set the gallon of maple syrup by the cooler to warm it.

Lastly, I lit the two camp cookers. I set the griddle on one and put bacon all along the upper edge. It would not only grease the griddle as the melting fat rolled across it, but the sizzling and the smell would bring the boys out of their beds. On the second camp cooker, I put a Dutch oven over each burner with some bacon in them to cook while greasing up the Dutch ovens.

Rod was up shortly after I was and headed out onto the ice to drill the holes. It wasn't long before I could hear the engine of the ice auger and see his silhouette against the dim morning light as he moved to different areas around the ice.

I mixed up a gallon pitcher full of pancake batter. As the bacon on the griddle shriveled, I dragged it across the griddle to grease it. Then I filled the griddle with good-sized, thick pancakes. I swirled the bacon in the Dutch ovens on the other camp cooker around the inside of the Dutch ovens, then cut those pieces into small bits. In the one Dutch oven, I cracked a couple dozen eggs and stirred them up with a bit of slushy, ice-crystalized milk. In the other Dutch oven, I dumped a bag full of hash browns.

By the time I flipped the first pancakes, the boys were beginning to wander out. Mort was first. He was shivering.

"Hey Mort," I said, handing him a ladle, "grab yourself a cup, spoon, and a packet of hot chocolate from the boxes on the table, and get some water from the Dutch oven on the fire."

Mort just nodded. He did as I said and was soon sipping a steaming cup of hot chocolate. The other boys saw what he had and followed suit as they came out. Jason was the last one out.

"How did you sleep?" I asked him as he wandered over to the fire to get warm.

"Oh, not as bad as I thought I would," he replied. "I could have been more comfortable in my nice, warm bed. But once Mort quit snoring, I slept okay."

"Hey, man, I don't snore," Mort shot back.

"Then it must have been the bear you got stuck in your throat that was growling," Gordy said.

"Oh, yeah," Mort replied. "Nothing could be as bad as your breath in my face all night. Did you swallow a skunk or were you just chewing on some of your old gym socks?"

"Ha, ha, ha," Gordy said, rolling his eyes. "Thousands of comedians out of work, and I get stuck with you."

It was my turn to roll my eyes. When Gordy got stuck on a phrase he would say it forever. I was sure we were going to hear that one a lot.

Sam, who seemed to have an insatiable curiosity, saw Rod drilling the holes in the ice and walked over to him. "Hey, could I try that?"

"It's not as easy as it looks," Rod said. "It takes a lot of force to keep the drill moving down."

"I would still like to try," Sam said.

Rod finished the hole he was working on; then they moved to a new spot that was near the camp. Rod got the drill started into the hole and then turned to Sam.

"Okay, Sam, just put all your weight on it and pull the throttle lever."

The auger had handles on both sides, with the throttle lever connected to one. Sam pushed down on the handles and pulled the throttle lever. The motor roared, and the auger spun, but it wasn't going down. It just seemed to spin around in the small hole Rod had started.

By this time, most of the boys had wandered over to Rod and Sam.

"You're not putting enough weight on it," Devin said.

"Brilliant deduction, Sherlock," Gordy replied.

"But that is all the weight I have," Sam said.

"Why don't you just lay across it?" Gordy asked. "That would put all of your weight on it."

They were just close enough that I could see a grin on Rod's face as he said, "Oh, that should be good."

Rod sounded sarcastic, but the boys, concentrating on Sam, didn't realize it. Sam seemed to think Rod was serious. Sam laid down across the auger and lifted his feet. Rod was grinning but made no move to stop Sam. Sam hit the throttle, and the auger didn't spin, but the handles did. Sam, on top of the handles, started spinning with them. The other boys jumped out of the road. Faster and faster Sam went until he was going at a dizzying speed.

I was sure Sam was going to be sick. "Sam, let go of the throttle," I yelled.

With bouncing, gurgling speech, Sam cried out, "I...I...I... c.a.n.'.t!"

No one dared jump in and try to stop Sam from spinning because it would probably hurt both of them. But then, suddenly, the auger churned into the ice and almost instantly cut through with Sam and the handles slamming down on top of the ice.

But still, Sam couldn't unlock his hands from the throttle, and the auger swirled water up onto the ice, soaking Sam and flooding the ice. It all happened so fast that the other boys didn't have a chance to move away. The water made the ice slick, and soon everyone was slipping and falling, except for Rod, who had had the good sense to move away in the first place.

Rod was able to reach up and pull Sam's hand from the throttle. And everything suddenly went quiet as the motor went back to idle. Rod helped Sam to his feet and, with a grin, turned to the other boys.

"Anybody else want a turn?"

They all shook their heads. "I think we're good," Jason said.

Sam and two others were wet enough that they had to change while Rod finished the rest of the holes. Soon all the boys were back sipping hot chocolate by the fire.

Rod finished the last hole and came back from the ice. He grabbed some hot chocolate, too.

By this time, the first batch of pancakes was stacked on the griddle, ready for anyone who wanted them. We had a blessing on the food, and I told everyone to grab their plates. Instead, the boys sat around shivering, sipping their hot chocolate.

"Well, if you boys aren't going to jump in and eat, I am," Rod said. "I'm ready to get out on the ice."

The hash browns and eggs were just finishing, so I filled up Rod's plate with the pancakes, eggs, and hash browns, with some bacon across the top. He poured on some syrup, which was barely warm enough to come out of the bottle, but still had the viscosity of twenty-weight motor oil. He poured himself a cup of slushy milk and sat down to eat.

Rod loved to fish, and it wasn't long before he had devoured the stack of food on his plate. He debated heading out to fish but decided he could stay on the ice longer if he didn't get hungry. He got a second helping. He had soon worked his way through that and was out on the ice before the first of the boys started wandering over from the fire.

Rod wasn't gone ten minutes before returning with a couple decent-sized fish. "You might as well throw these on the grill while you're cooking."

I don't think he was as worried about frying up the fish as getting the boys moving. At the sight of the fish, everything in the camp changed. Suddenly, all the boys were in line trying to get their share of food. The eggs and hash browns disappeared quickly, and I had to replenish them. The boys were clamoring for the pancakes off the grill even before the pancakes were half-cooked.

When Gordy grabbed the spatula and flipped a couple of only slightly browned pancakes onto his plate, I laughed.

"Those are what I call Twinkie cakes," I told him.

"Twinkie cakes?" he asked.

"Yes. Lightly brown on the outside, but cream filled on the inside."

It seemed like hardly any time at all before everyone else had eaten and had moved out to their holes on the ice. The one that surprised me most was Jason. He was more at home with computers than with fish. He hated worms and the sliminess of fish when he caught them. But the intrigue of putting the line into a hole in the ice and pulling something out seemed to excite him.

I cooked myself a good batch of food and took a nice leisurely time to eat it. My story from the night before still filled my mind, and the thought of being on that cold mountain with no food made the current breakfast all that much more enjoyable. As I ate, I watched as Rod caught fish after fish, and the boys caught nothing.

Even after I finished eating and was cleaning up, I could see the same results playing out on the ice.

I put the extra pancakes, eggs, and hash browns in Dutch ovens by the fire to stay warm in case the boys wanted something later. I was just finishing when I saw Mike walk up to Rod.

"Hey, Rod," Mike said. "You are the only one catching fish. Can I trade places with you?"

Rod nodded and went over to Mike's fishing spot. Soon Rod was pulling fish out of Mike's old fishing hole, and Mike was pulling nothing out of the one Rod had given him.

Next, Seth approached Rod about switching spots with him. Again, Rod switched. Then I watched Rod pulling fish out of Seth's old spot, and Seth pulling nothing out of his new one.

This happened a couple more times with other boys. Rod had probably already surpassed his limit on fish, but that didn't seem to slow him down. He said he would just let some of the boys count what he caught as part of theirs.

Finally, Gordy put down his pole and came over to Rod just as Rod was pulling out another fish.

"Rod," Gordy said, "how come you seem to pull fish out of any hole you fish in, and the rest of us can't?"

By this time, all the boys had gathered around Rod.

Dallin laughed. "Well, you know, Gordy, in your case, it's understandable. The fish look up through the hole in the ice, see your face, and it scares them away."

"Ha, ha, ha," Gordy said. "Thousands of comedians out of work, and I get stuck with you."

The boys then turned back to Rod. "Yeah, why is it, Rod,

that you can catch fish wherever you go, but we can't?" Sam asked.

Rod put his hand to his mouth, spit into his hand, then held his hand open for the boys to look into. "You see, boys, the fish like warm, wiggly worms. You need to keep your worms in your mouth so they can stay warm and fresh, not cold and frozen in a bait can."

The looks on the boys' faces were priceless. I thought Jason was going to lose his breakfast. But what made me smile even more was something I saw from my position that the boys didn't. When Rod put his hand over his mouth, he actually reached the bottom two fingers into a little pouch just inside his shirt. It was from this pouch that he had pulled the worms, not from his mouth.

The boys looked at each other, then back at Rod. They all then moved back to their fishing holes.

I wondered if the boys would actually put the worms in their mouths. I shouldn't have wondered. They were scouts, after all.

Soon, every boy had worms in his mouth, and they all started to catch fish. Having worms in a person's mouth does make them warm and wiggly. But so would a nice pouch against someone's throat.

But now, with the boys having the worms in their mouths, they were right where Rod wanted them. He walked from boy to boy, slapping them on the back as if he was being friendly. Each boy, in turn, swallowed the worms. When Rod slapped Gordy on the back, Gordy started to cough and gag. When he got himself together, he looked with wide eyes at Rod.

"You made me swallow my worms!"

"Oh, no problem," Rod said. "I'll go get you some more."

Rod returned to camp and got some worms from the supply I had purchased. He took a couple of big ones to Gordy.

"Here you go. They are nice and fresh. I didn't even wash the dirt off them."

16
Confrontation

With David off to college in September, Alex came by himself to campouts. But without David to get him to the weekly scout meetings, he came later and later. In the spring, he started missing meetings now and then.

Some of the boys told me that Alex had started hanging with the wrong crowd and taking Sam with him. Marissa had expressed her concern about Sam, and I had long talks with both boys while we were camping. I was doing what I could, but as Alex started missing more and more meetings, I decided to pay him a visit. So, one night, before the scout meeting, I went to see if he would like a ride.

Not long after I knocked on the door, Mrs. Handon answered. When I asked to visit with Alex, she nodded. Before she could call Alex, Mr. Handon yelled out in a drunk voice from farther in the house. "Nan, who is it?"

"It's Mr. Johnson," she called back.

"Well, tell that sissy scout leader we're not interested in having him here," Mr. Handon yelled.

Mrs. Handon seemed embarrassed. "He's here to talk to Alex," she called back. She then called, "Alex, Mr. Johnson is here to see you."

As I waited, apparently Alex passed by where his father was because suddenly Mr. Handon yelled, "So, are you going off to sissy scouts? Trying to be better than your old man, are you? I'm not good enough for you, am I?"

I couldn't hear any of Alex's reply to his father. But when he came to the door, he hung his head and just looked at the floor.

"Hi, Alex," I said, acting like I hadn't heard anything. "You used to come to scouts all the time when David was here and brought you. I just wondered if you would like a ride."

"Go be a girlie camper if you want, Alex," Mr. Handon yelled from the other room. "I don't want to stop you if that's what you want to be."

Alex didn't look up as he said, "I don't think I can go. Maybe another time."

I reached out my hand, and he shook it but never looked up. "We miss having you there," I said. "I hope you can join us soon."

As I went away, I wondered if I had done more harm than good. I didn't mean to put Alex in an awkward situation with his father. I had tried at times to reach out to Mr. Handon, but never had any luck.

Alex didn't come for a while, and I didn't think it was good for me to go over there to do anything about it. But about a month after the episode I had with Mr. Handon, the weather had warmed enough that we moved our scout meeting outside. We were working on the physical fitness merit badge, and I felt the fresh air would do us all some good. I was pleased when I saw David drive up, and he had Alex with him.

Alex climbed out to join us, and David rolled down the window to visit. "I heard what my dad said the evening you came over. I was home this week from college, and I thought I'd bring Alex over to scouts."

"Why don't you join us for the evening?" I asked.

"Is it okay with me being older, graduated, and out of scouts?"

"Sure," I replied. "The boys would love to have you here. They really look up to you."

David parked his car and came over to where we were. It was fun to have him there. We started working through the physical fitness things when a pickup pulled in, the radio blaring with a bass that made the ground shake at every pounding beat. The four young men who stepped from it were dressed louder than the radio played.

They had enough piercings to qualify as acupuncture poster children, and chains dangled from the fake leather they were attired in. Their swagger quickly told me they were not there for scouts.

The other boys had told me who Alex and Sam were hanging out with, and I immediately recognized the group's leader. I did not know him personally, but he was the perfect likeness to his father. He was a Dalton. The Daltons were a tough group that was known to sometimes be bullies. They were also known for motorcycle gangs, not the scout law. I had been told his name was Kalmin, but he went by Kal.

Alex and Sam stepped up to greet him. Kal smirked at them. "So, Alex, your old man told me you were over here at sissy scouts. I didn't know I would find Sam here, too."

Sam and Alex looked embarrassed.

David bristled. "Go away, Kal, and leave Alex and Sam alone."

Kal turned to Alex and spoke in a patronizing tone. "Oh, Alex, are you letting your big brother tell you what to do?" Kal then turned to David. "You aren't at the high school anymore, David. You can't tell us what to do. We're the ones in charge there now."

The other boys with Kal laughed.

"So, Kal," I said, "we're doing physical fitness tonight. Do you want to join us?"

Kal smirked. "Do we look like we need physical fitness?"

As Kal's friends laughed, Gordy said, "With all of your piercings, it looks like you need to avoid magnets at all costs."

The grin on Kal's face left him. "You speak pretty smart, Hider, you punk. You better be able to back your arrogant words."

Kal and those with him stepped toward Gordy, and I stepped in front of him. "If you don't want to join us tonight, Kal, we need to get back to our meeting, and you need to leave."

He eyed me like he was sizing me up. "You talk pretty tough for an old man. And how do you know my name? You talk as if you knew it before anyone else even said it."

"I don't know you personally, but I know your father," I replied. "We went to high school together."

"What's your name?" Kal asked.

"My name is Tom," I said, holding out my hand.

He didn't take my hand, but looked at me as if thinking. "Tom? Are you Tom Johnson?"

I nodded. "Yes."

"I can't believe it," he replied. "I have heard a lot about you. I heard how you were like unbeatable in high school. I heard how you beat my father in wrestling when you were just a sophomore. My old man talks about you like you're folklore."

"I wasn't unbeatable. In fact, Rand beat me once in wrestling himself," I replied.

"Even if he did," Kal said, "he says you beat him really bad once, and that is why he quit the wrestling team. My old man is such a quitter."

"He's not a quitter," I replied. "He quit the team because the coach forced him to do something he didn't want to do to drive me from the team. That might be why I fought so hard and, as you say, beat him so well. But Rand is an honorable man and was upset about the whole situation, not because of losing."

"My old man, honorable," Kal said. "That's rich. And look at you. You're just an old man now, too. You couldn't beat anyone."

"He could kick your butt every day of the week and twice on Sunday," Gordy said.

I turned to Gordy. "Gordy, we don't need that right now."

"Well, I'll tell you what," Kal said to Gordy, "if he can kick my butt, then I will leave and not kick yours." Kal then turned to me. "How about it, old man?"

"I've been trying to teach the boys that physical toughness is not the best way to deal with any issue," I replied.

"Okay," Kal said. "I understand if you're scared. I'll just kick Hider's butt instead."

"I'm not scared, nor am I going to let you touch one of these young men," I replied.

"Then it's a challenge," Kal said. "I've become a tough wrestler myself. And I've wanted to wrestle you ever since I heard my father talk about you."

I shrugged. "Whatever."

"Since we don't have a mat," Kal said, "let's go three falls out of five."

Kal took off his jacket and his shirt. He had tattoos on both arms and his chest. He looked at me as if expecting me to do the same.

"I'll leave my shirt on," I said.

Everyone formed a wide circle around us. Kal and I circled each other. He would jump at me as if he was trying to scare me, and then he'd laugh. But it seemed to annoy him that I didn't take the bait and jump away.

"You don't respond to stupid movements," my college coach used to say. "You watch their waist. The waist dictates the true movement of their whole body."

And I knew Kal's jumping wasn't true attack movements. If they were, he would be too off balance.

I did, however, watch him carefully. One thing he was right about was that I was older, and I needed to be more careful.

Suddenly, he shot in. I immediately dropped all my weight on him, and it slammed him face-first into the grass. I may have been older, but I was also much heavier, and I planned to use it to my advantage. Once he was down, I swung around behind him and put my arm tightly around his waist so he couldn't move. I just put all my weight on him and held him there until he said, "Okay, you got one."

"See, I told you," Gordy said.

"Gordy!" I said, and he went quiet.

Kal and I both stood and moved into position across from each other. He didn't try any of his little jumps at me now, and he was watching me intently. As we moved in closer, Kal shot in, but this time he kept his body more upright so I couldn't force him down. I dropped and sprawled enough to stop his momentum. I pushed his head down and spun behind him, then I grabbed him around the waist and cinched my arm tight until he gasped for air. I lifted him off his feet, and, turning him, brought him down sideways with me on top of him. Once more, I held him until he said, "Okay."

As Kal stood, he was still breathing hard. "My dad said you had a grip like iron. Now I see what he means."

Rod had been quiet until now, letting me handle the challenge. But now he said, "That's two."

"I know what it is!" Kal yelled. "And that's his last."

I saw Kal nod to a couple of his friends, and they moved so they were on each side of me. Kal didn't circle, but stepped back and forth. I'm sure it was obvious to more than just me that his two friends planned to help him. I tried to keep them in my peripheral vision. The instant Kal shot in, so did they. But I had been watching his waist and anticipated his move. I beat him by microseconds, shooting in under him before his friends reached me. He tried to sprawl on me as his friends grabbed at me, but I pulled Kal into a fireman's carry and picked him clear up off the ground. Then I set him down on his back and held him there, with his friends pulling at my arms. But their tugging at me in opposing directions did nothing to pull me off of Kal.

"That's three," Rod said.

I still held Kal there until he said, "Okay."

Kal stood, and so did his two friends.

"Tom beat you fair and square, even though you tried to cheat," David said.

"Shut up, Handon!" Kal said.

Kal then turned to Alex and Sam. "We came to get you two so you won't have to stay at Sissy scouts. You coming?"

Alex swung his head toward David, as if trying to tell Kal he didn't dare go while David was there. Sam just looked away.

"All right," Kal said. "Enjoy being sissies!"

He and his friends went to the pickup. Soon the engine roared, and Kal spun the tires, leaving black smoke and the stench of burning rubber. As he turned the pickup, he spun it onto the church lawn and revved the engine. The tires dug big trenches into the lawn, throwing dirt halfway across the parking lot. But soon, the sound of the roaring engine faded in the distance.

As I stood there contemplating what had happened, it felt like the entire episode had lasted for hours, though it had only been about twenty minutes.

Gordy said, "Well, I guess you sure showed him."

I turned to him and said, "Gordy, you know what? I really didn't want to show anyone anything. It's one thing to compete in an athletic competition, and it is completely another to use strength as just happened. Being stronger than someone else doesn't make you better than them; it just makes you stronger. Being smarter, faster, or tougher doesn't make you better than someone; it only makes you smarter, faster, or tougher. Everyone is better than somebody else in something. That doesn't make them better than another person except in that thing."

"Wow. That was deep," Rod said.

I sighed. "Maybe we should just cancel the rest of the meeting and go play basketball."

The boys liked that idea, and they headed in to play. Rod waited until they were gone. Then he turned to me. "Something's wrong, isn't it?"

I nodded. "Rod, I keep trying to teach these boys the scout values—trustworthy, loyal, helpful, friendly, etc. But things like this seem to say all that matters is being tough."

"But you couldn't let him and his mob hurt Gordy. You showed that it's important to stick up for others."

I nodded. "I suppose that's true. But I wonder what events like wrestling at the Conclave Games, throwing Gordy in the stream, or accepting this challenge with Kal are actually teaching the boys."

"Well, for what it's worth, I think you did the right thing," Rod said.

"I hope so," I replied.

We went into the church, and Rod went to play ball with the boys. I found the bishop and told him what had happened. He seemed to feel like Rod did, that what I had done needed to be done. It made me feel better.

I went to join in the basketball game, and Rod pulled me aside.

"While you were in visiting with the bishop, the boys told me something. You don't have to worry about that group actually picking on Gordy. Apparently, that Kal kid and his friends were bluffing because Gordy has so many athlete friends at school that they know they would be in trouble if they did anything to him."

"That's good to know," I replied.

I joined the others and was really off my game. I couldn't hit anything, and my team lost badly.

"It's good you didn't challenge Kal in basketball," Gordy said.

Mort nodded. "You were right. No one is perfect at everything."

Basketball helped, and by the time we went home, I felt better.

17
Something is Wrong

The next scout night, Alex and Sam didn't come. I kept thinking that at least Sam would show up anytime because he never missed. But after a half hour, I sensed that something must be wrong.

I left Rod in charge of working with the boys on their physical fitness merit badge, and I went to call Marissa. When she answered, I said, "Hi, Marissa. This is Tom at scouts. I was wondering if Sam was sick since he didn't show up."

There was panic in her voice as she answered. "He should be there! Alex came over about an hour before scouts, and he and Sam were going to walk to the church. I have been trying to curtail the time Sam spends with Alex because I have felt Alex was leading Sam to things they shouldn't do. But I thought it would be okay if they were going to scouts."

I told her I was going to go look for them. She decided she was also going to call the sheriff's office to have them search. We both had bad feelings about this.

I talked to the bishop and explained the situation. He said he would join Rod to help be backup with the scouts. Then I left.

First, I drove along the road between the church and Marissa's house. It was less than a mile, and two boys could walk it in about fifteen minutes. I hoped that they had found something of interest that had detained them. I drove slowly along the road, looking carefully, but there was no sign of them.

When I reached Marissa's house, she rushed out to meet me. I could see the fear on her face.

"Marissa, do you have any idea where they might be?" I asked.

"I'm sure they're with that rough kid Alex has become friends with," she replied.

"Are you talking about Kal Dalton?"

She nodded. "I do think his name was Kal. Do you know him?"

"I had a run-in with him last week at scouts when he tried to come and get Alex and Sam."

"I forbade Sam from having anything to do with that kid and his group," Marissa said. "That is why I didn't let him spend much time with Alex."

She looked like she might pass out as the tears started pouring down her face. I helped her back to her porch, and she sat down on the steps.

"Do you have any idea where they might have gone?" I asked. She shook her head, so I asked, "Is there any place Sam has talked about?"

She paused for a moment, then nodded. "He has talked about a lake where teenagers like to go. He said they roasted marshmallows and stuff, but I got the feeling they did more than that and told him he couldn't go. I can't remember the name."

"I know where it is," I said. "It's called Pheasant Lake. I'll head out there."

I got back in my pickup and headed on my way. It was only about five miles to the lake. It was well known for teenage partying. Marissa was right to have concerns about it. It had a bad reputation for drinking and wild parties there. Most of the locals avoided it.

When I pulled in, I saw a bunch of teenagers around a few different fires. My eyes were drawn to a group that instantly became very active when they saw me. It looked to me like they were trying to hide some things. I thought it was likely beer that they were too young to be drinking legally.

I walked along the beach from group to group, hoping to see Alex and Sam, but they weren't there. When I got to the group that had looked like they were hiding things, I didn't find the two boys, but I recognized three of the young men there as the three that had been with Kal the week before.

"Hi," I said. "I'm looking for someone."

At least one of the young men must have recognized me because he said, "One of your scouts?"

"Yes," I replied. "Actually, two of them. Alex and Sam."

The biggest of the three young men said, "And even if we had seen them, why would we tell you? It's not like anyone is doing anything wrong just being here."

I could smell alcohol and figured some of them were probably underage to be drinking. But I thought that it was not a good time to bring that up if I wanted their help.

"That's a good question," I replied. "You have no reason to help me. But Alex's mother thought they might come here. She's planning to call the sheriff's office. I was hoping to find them before the sheriff needed to."

I could see by the look on their faces that I had struck a chord. The last thing they wanted was to talk to anyone in law enforcement. The young men looked back and forth at each other for a moment, then one of them spoke.

"Okay, they were here. Alex and Sam left with Kal in Kal's truck."

"Do you have any idea where they might have gone?" I asked.

The young man shook his head, and another one answered. "Sam was concerned about getting back in time so that his mother wouldn't worry. They were going to have a bit of fun, drag main, do some off-roading, or zip around some country roads. Nothing bad."

We talked for another few minutes, but they didn't have any more they could add. I was turning to leave when a sheriff's deputy that I knew from my high school years walked up.

"Hello, Tom. Sam's mother said I might find you here. Any word?"

I nodded. "A little. These young men said Alex and Sam were here, but they went off with Kal in his pickup truck. They planned to drag main, off-road a little, or zip around country roads. That's about all they know."

The deputy turned to the young men. "Is there anything else you can tell us?"

They all shook their heads. If they seemed reluctant to talk to me, they were even more so with the deputy. I'm sure he could also smell the alcohol, but he didn't mention it, either. Maybe he felt it wasn't the time, too. He just told them it was getting late and they might want to get home. He asked them if any of them needed a ride, and they all shook their heads.

As he and I walked away, I remembered something else. "There was one other thing they said that I forgot. Sam was concerned about getting home before his mother worried about him. So those young men said they planned to be home before she knew anything different than that he was at scouts. That worries me that something happened."

The deputy nodded. "I'll put out a notice and have our officers keep an eye out for them."

"Do you need a description of the vehicle?" I asked.

The deputy laughed. He gave me a perfect description of Kal's pickup, then laughed again. "This isn't the first time we've had to look for that vehicle and its occupants."

"Is there anything I can do?" I asked.

"If you can think of any other place they might have gone, you might check it out," he replied. "I think that maybe they haven't made it back because they went off-roading and got stuck. At least, I hope that's the reason."

When I left there, I went home and told Hannah why I was late getting home from scouts. Grabbing a flashlight, I said, "I'm going to go out and check some of the dirt roads around here to see if I can find them."

"Be careful," she said.

"Don't worry," I replied. I will stay on solid roads.

I followed many of the country dirt roads until they came to dead ends. I looked for any tire tracks that might go off from there.

159

Most did not look like they had been traveled recently. I did find one set of tracks leading off the road that looked fresh. I didn't dare follow them in my little pickup, so I got out and walked along the tracks. I walked about a mile before they ended at a campfire ring. But there was no pickup, so I walked back.

After I checked every dirt road I could think of in our community, I drove around all the paved roads in the area. I then turned toward home. It was just after midnight. When I got there, I asked Hannah if there was any word.

She shook her head. "Not that they have been found, anyway. Sam's mother called. She said she called the Handon's. Alex's mom didn't know anything, but Mr. Handan knew Alex wasn't really headed to scouts and had been okay with it. But now they're both worried, too."

I called Marissa, and she also told me the boys had not been found yet. She was so emotional she could hardly speak. "The deputy told me to get some sleep, and they would let me know if they found out anything. But there's no way I can sleep."

"I don't know what else I can do right now," I said. "I think I'll try to get some sleep, and then I'll take the day off tomorrow and keep looking."

After we hung up, I went to bed, but it took me a long time to calm my mind in order to sleep. And when I finally slept, it was broken by strange dreams.

18
A Terrible Accident

I woke up, but I couldn't figure out what woke me. Then the phone rang, and I realized it had rung before, which was why I was awake. Hanna answered it with a slurred hello. After a moment, she spoke into the receiver again. "Yes, he's here."

I sat up to take the call so I could try to get my senses about me. As soon as I said hello, I heard the bishop's voice on the other end. "Tom, there's been an accident. Alex was killed, and Sam is in the hospital in critical condition."

Instantly, I was fully alert. He told me that the sheriff had called him and told him about it at Marissa's request, and she had asked that he contact me. He felt it would we should got to the hospital. He didn't know all the details but said he'd meet me there.

I swallowed hard to remove the pain in my heart that was building as I tried to explain to Hannah what had happened and where I was going. I dressed quickly and headed on my way. As I stepped into the cool morning air, I felt as if someone had slugged me, not from the crispness of it, but more because of the realization of what had happened to two of my boys.

My mind kept trying to make sense of it and confront the reality of what I now knew to be the truth, though my heart refused to believe it. It was a long twenty-minute drive to the hospital as my thoughts and pain wore on me.

The only entrance open was at the emergency room. I went to the desk and told them who I was and that I was there to see Sam Fredricks. The woman typed some things into the computer before looking up. "I'm afraid that since he is in ICU that only family is allowed to visit."

I explained further that I was his scout leader and was like family. She looked dubious but said she would call his room and see what his mother said. After a brief conversation on the phone, she hung up and turned to me. "She asked that you be allowed in. He is in wing C, room 224."

I quickly made my way down the hallway. When I finally found the room, I stopped. I didn't know how Marissa would receive me. She did ask that I be allowed to come down, but I didn't know if she would feel it was my fault that he had not come to scouts the night before. I took a few deep breaths, steeled myself, then walked in.

I wasn't ready for the sight that met my eyes. Sam lay still on the bed, multiple tubes attached to him. At the sound of the door, Marissa turned. Her tear-stained face spoke volumes. She stood but said nothing, just looking at me, and I wondered what she was thinking. Suddenly, she rushed to me, throwing herself into my arms, sobbing. I felt awkward as I held her, but I felt my own tears rolling down my face, and grief lessens when it is shared.

When Marissa's tears subsided, she pulled back from me. "I'm sorry. I just..."

I patted her shoulder. "It's okay. I understand."

She tried to smile. "You're the closest to a father he's ever known."

"I have felt all of the boys were like my own sons," I replied

"He loves scouts, and he loves you."

I felt such guilt sweep over me. "But he wasn't at scouts last night. If he had, this wouldn't have happened."

Marissa took my hand in hers. "It's not your fault. I knew he was starting to have some of the wrong friends at school. I've tried to keep him from spending time with them, and so have you. If it weren't for scouts, he would have been with them far more than he has been."

My voice choked as I tried to reply. "But he is lying here in critical condition, and Alex is gone."

She nodded and spoke kindly. "But you did all you could."

We sat down to talk, and she continued speaking kindly to me. I had come to try and be a support to her, and yet I found myself gaining more strength from her than I was giving. As we visited, the bishop arrived. Marissa hugged him and thanked him for coming. We all talked. We learned from Marissa that besides Alex and Sam, two other boys were in the pickup. One was Kal, and the other was another boy from their group whom I hadn't met. Marissa couldn't remember his name. She said she heard that boy had a broken leg, and Kal only had a couple of cuts and abrasions and had been treated and released.

As we continued to talk, the sheriff walked in. He knew the Bishop and Marissa, though he wasn't acquainted with me. He said he had more information about the accident and looked at me as if he wasn't sure he should speak with me there. Marissa seemed to understand the sheriff's reluctance.

"It's okay. Tom is the boys' scoutmaster. It would be good for both the bishop and him to hear whatever you have to share."

The sheriff said the initial investigation showed that Alex had been driving. He said the fourth boy, the one with a broken leg, was named Zane. It was Kal's pickup, but Alex had wanted to drive it, and the other boys decided that since Alex had brought the beer, they should let him. He said all evidence pointed to the fact that Alex truly was driving. The indication was that in his drunken state, he had gotten one wheel off the road and had overcorrected and rolled the pickup. They must have been going very fast because they rolled multiple times out into a field. They ended up a long distance from the road, which was why no one saw them for a long time.

The sheriff explained that there would be a thorough investigation, especially since the boys were all underage. "If Alex was able to purchase the alcohol at some store, there could be criminal charges filed. The place or person from which he got the beer is in a big part responsible."

He then turned to the bishop. "I don't know if you have someone you can ask to visit with the Handons. As soon as my deputy informed them that their son had been killed, he was thrown out of the house by Mr. Handon, who started yelling and threatening to shoot half the people in the county. It might be good if there was someone you felt could talk with him and calm him down before he does something stupid."

The bishop turned to me. "How about you, Tom? You seem to get in there at least as well as anybody."

A twinge of fear came over me as I thought of my episode with Mr. Handon when I asked for Alex and David to be in scouts. "I'm not sure I'm the best. He definitely doesn't view me as his friend."

"The only people he views as his friends," the bishop said, "are his drinking buddies. And they would be more likely to inflame him than to calm him down."

"I'm not sure he will let me in."

"Since this is about Alex, he is more likely to let you in than anyone else I can think of." The bishop paused and looked directly at me. "I'd really like you to try."

I promised I would, though my heart trembled at the thought. The sheriff visited a while longer, but my mind was caught up with the thoughts of that future visit with Mr. Handon, and I couldn't concentrate on anything else that was said.

After the sheriff left, Marissa started to talk. She talked about how she did not like Mr. Handon and didn't like her son visiting their house. Even though Alex was driving, what bitterness she seemed to feel was directed more at his father. She admitted that it might be partially because of her unpleasant experience with her husband, but she still didn't like him.

We talked for a long time. When Marissa came to the hospital, a woman in the community had come over to watch the other children. The bishop said he would talk to the women to ensure Marissa's children were always cared for. I told him that I was sure Hannah would be willing to help, too.

We were still visiting when the doctor walked in. He questioned Marissa about sharing information in front of the bishop and me, and she graciously said we were like family. It was a good report. The doctor said that Sam's vital signs were good, and he was sure he would recover. He said he would be in a wheelchair for some time because both legs were broken, but, excluding some unforeseen problems, he felt Sam would recover fully and quickly.

After the doctor left, we briefly visited again. We had a prayer together, a blessing for Sam, and then the bishop and I prepared to leave. As I was leaving, the bishop put his hand on my shoulder. "Good luck talking to Mr. Handon, Tom. We'll be praying for you. And thank you."

As I walked to my car, I felt the soberness of the assignment that had been asked of me. I went home and tried to get some sleep with what few hours I had left, but sleep was far from me.

I decided to go to work, hoping to get my mind off of what I had to do, but the assignment ate at me all day while I was there. As soon as work was over, I headed over to the Handons' home. I didn't want to do it, but I had to get it over with.

As I approached their door, I could feel my heart racing wildly. I paused only briefly before I knocked, knowing time would not make it easier. It was a long time before anyone answered, and I began to think no one was home, though I could hear noise inside. Finally, the door opened slightly. Mrs. Handon's face appeared, and I could see immediately that her eyes were swollen and red. She forced a smile and opened the door wide, inviting me in.

Mr. Handon sat in a big easy chair, beer in hand, staring at the television that was blaring loudly. He looked up at me and scowled. "What are you doing here?"

"I came to express my condolences about Alex."

"This wouldn't have happened if you had been a decent scoutmaster so he would have been at scouts instead of somewhere else."

That comment both cut and angered me at the same time. I knew how much he had fought Alex on coming to scouts. I also knew he had given Alex his blessing to skip scouts that night. And now he was blaming me for Alex not having been there. I swallowed hard to hold back my anger, knowing it wouldn't help. Even so, I felt I needed to say something in my defense. "Alex said you didn't like scouts."

"I never said I didn't like scouts. I didn't want you making a sissy out of my son."

"I viewed Alex and all the boys as if they were my sons."

"Yeah, right," he snarled. "If you had been half a man, he would have preferred being at scouts instead of off somewhere else."

David, whom I learned had come home from college because of Alex's death, spoke strongly to his father. "Dad, you know you can't blame Tom. You often told Alex only a girl would be a scout."

Mr. Handon turned angrily to his son. "You shut up and mind your own business! Besides," Mr. Handon continued, reaching down beside his chair and picking up a gun he had sitting there, "the one I really blame is the one who was driving. He is the one that took the life of my son. When I find out who it was, I will put a bullet through his head."

"The sheriff said it was Alex who was driving," I said.

Mr. Handon waved his gun menacingly at me. "That's a bunch of crap, and you know it! Why would he be driving? It wasn't our car."

"The sheriff said the other boys told him that Alex begged to drive, and since he had been the one to bring the beer, they let him. The sheriff said they were doing more investigating, especially since the boys were all underage and it was illegal for them to have alcohol. He said if they could find out from whom or from where Alex was able to get the beer, they might file some criminal charges, because that store or that person he got the beer from was at least partially responsible for Alex's death."

Suddenly, everyone in the room went quiet. All the rest of the family turned and looked at Mr. Handon, and his face flushed red with anger. Why it had never crossed my mind before, I don't know. Perhaps it was because my grief kept me from thinking clearly, but it suddenly hit me where Alex got the beer. He got it from his home—from the supply his father kept.

Suddenly, I also realized the dangerous position I had just put myself in. I was in the home of a drunken man who seemed to be, at least partially, blaming me for his son's death and threatening anyone he felt had anything to do with it.

The silence in the room was palpable as everyone else stared at Mr. Handon. I didn't dare look at him directly but turned my gaze in turn to Mrs. Handon and David. The silence, though brief, seemed eternal and ominous. When I finally looked at Mr. Handon, I could see the anger burning in his eyes. "Get out of my home!" he shouted. "Get out before I put a bullet through your head. You're the reason my son is dead, and you come here making accusations!"

"I didn't mean..."

He cut me off as he raised the gun, pointed it directly at me, and shouted louder. "Just get out!"

Mrs. Handon touched my arm and nodded, and I could see the fear in her eyes. I wasn't sure Mr. Handon wouldn't do as he said, and I could see she wasn't either. Mrs. Handon led me to the door and opened it for me.

I turned back one more time. "I want you to know I really did love Alex as if he were my own son."

Mr. Handon slammed down his beer bottle, breaking it into shards and sending beer everywhere. He then stood and pointed the gun in my direction again. "Get out! Now!"

As I stepped out the door, Mrs. Handon touched my arm. "I'm sorry," she whispered before closing the door behind me.

The instant the door closed I could hear Mr. Handon yelling. "Who does that miserable excuse for a scoutmaster think he is? If he was halfway decent, my son would have been at scouts and would be alive right now. How dare he come here accusing others when he's as much at fault as anyone?"

I could hear David's voice, angry in reply. "Father, he is a great scoutmaster. And you always made fun of Alex for going to scouts. And you know darned well where Alex got the alcohol."

Again, I heard Mr. Handon's voice thunder out. "I thought I told you to shut up and mind your own business!"

I could hear the yelling continue as I made my way to my pickup. As I climbed in and drove away, my mind was swirling with thoughts of what had just happened. Mr. Handon said he would put a bullet through the head of any man who cost his son's life, and yet, in essence, he was the one responsible. He had fought his son in going to scouts. He had kept the beer so prominently in his home where his son had access to it. Alex had even told me his father had invited him to drink with him on some evenings. Yet, with all of that, he blamed me.

My mind returned to what Marissa had told Hannah. Mr. Handon knew Alex wasn't going to scouts that night and was okay with it. Did Alex sneak the beer away, or did Mr. Handon give it to him? Many thoughts swirled through my mind as my heart struggled with the feelings.

I knew Mr. Handon's anger was actually because he had no one else to blame, yet I still felt perhaps some of the blame truly could be mine. Maybe if I hadn't been so strong with Kal and those with him. I just felt that I needed to protect my boys.

Perhaps I should have tried to reach out to Kal and his friends more. I started questioning about what if I had done this, or what if I had done that, would Alex still be alive? The doubts and questions came so strong and fast that by the time I pulled into my driveway, I felt that Mr. Handon was right about one thing. I was a poor excuse for a scoutmaster. And as that feeling overwhelmed me, I pulled my pickup to a stop, laid my head on the steering wheel, closed my eyes, and felt the pain burn through my heart.

19

Blame and Responsibility

$\mathbb{T}$ he night of the viewing was overcast and drizzly. It seems that funeral days tend to be that way. Maybe they aren't any more than any other day, but they seem to be. Perhaps it's just that our moods and feelings are that way, so it magnifies the slightest tendency of the weather in that direction.

Nonetheless, by the time I arrived at the funeral home, my spirit was about as low as I ever remember it being in my life. I came early, hoping to go through quickly. As I walked through the family line, I shook David's hand, and he gave me a big hug. The family seemed happy to see me there, all, of course, except for Mr. Handon. He refused to shake my hand, scowled, and turned away from me. He didn't say anything, however, even when Mrs. Handon hugged me and thanked me for all I had done for Alex, though his scowl increased dramatically. I could tell he preferred I wasn't there.

I looked at Alex in the coffin. I was surprised to see him dressed in his scout uniform. I became emotional when I saw it. Mrs. Handon saw the tears in my eyes and hugged me again. "We knew he would have wanted to be buried in it."

I couldn't speak, so I just nodded and turned to leave, but when I stepped outside, I realized David had followed me. He touched my shoulder, and I turned back. He smiled kindly. "I want you to know that none of the family blames you. Father may try to place the blame somewhere else, but it's only because he knows it's really his own fault. The rest of the family is angry with how he treated you. It's the first time that our family has stood halfway united against Father, even insisting Alex be buried in his scout uniform."

He patted my arm. "I want you to know that we all know

you did so much for Alex and me, and Alex loved scouting and you and Rod, just as all of us boys do."

I thanked him for his kind words and then turned to leave as he rejoined his family. My heart was heavy, and I needed to be alone. With all the kind words, there still lingered in my heart the feeling that I should have done more.

As I came to the church, I pulled in and sought the solitude of the scout room. I sat in a chair and looked up at the pictures of my boys smiling out at me from our bulletin board. There were pictures at courts-of-honor, campouts, hikes, and even a few from nights at the church. My eyes scanned over Alex and Sam. I felt I had failed them, and I couldn't hold the pain in my heart any longer. I laid my head on my arms on the table and could not hold back the tears. I grew up being told that real men don't cry, and yet, in the quiet stillness when I was alone, my love for my boys tore at my heart until I needed a release from the pain I felt.

When the tears had washed away some of the pain, I sat up and wiped my eyes. I sat there in the stillness for a long time, just feeling numb. I don't know how much time had passed when I heard the door click. It opened, and there stood the bishop. He smiled, but I couldn't return one of my own. Instead, I turned away as I spoke. "I suppose you came to tell me that you and the committee would like to release me from being scoutmaster?"

"No. In fact, just the opposite." He pulled up a chair and sat across the table from me, though I still could not look at him as he continued. "I thought I might find you here, and I was concerned you might be having those kinds of feelings. But I want you to know that you have the confidence of everyone in this community."

"Not everyone. Mr. Handon blames me for Alex's death."

I heard a slight tone of anger as the bishop spoke of Mr. Handon. "He knows very well it's not your fault. Everyone knows that if there is anyone to blame, it's Mr. Handon himself."

The bishop had called the night after I had visited with Handons to see how it went, and I had told him everything. But even though he also knew of what had happened in scouts the week

Kal and his friends had come, I again recounted it and finished by saying, "I just feel I could have handled it better. Perhaps if I had, Alex would have been at scouts on Tuesday and would still be alive."

The bishop spoke kindly but firmly. "Tom?" I looked up at him, and he continued. "You did what you needed to do. You couldn't allow those other boys to come around and cause problems. Everyone knows that you have put your heart and soul into leading and helping these boys. You will always have the full support of myself, the other church leaders, the scout committee, and most of all, the parents."

The bishop paused for some time and then spoke thoughtfully. "You cannot make the boys' choices for them nor take away their agency. Even God wouldn't do that. It wouldn't be good for them if you could. And part of allowing them the agency to make their own decisions is allowing them the agency to fail and face the consequences of the decisions they make."

I just nodded. I had often talked to the boys about agency around the campfire, but somehow it sounded different when the application showed a side of it I would rather not see. The bishop seemed to sense the deep inner struggle I felt. He patted my arm once more. "We really want you to continue being the scoutmaster."

I turned my eyes away again, struggling to hold my emotions. "I'm just not sure how effective I can be with how I feel."

He stood and prepared to leave. "I understand, and the decision ultimately has to be yours. But know that we are behind you and know you have done and still can do much for the boys. Besides, what would the boys do without you? They would miss you a lot."

He left me to ponder that, and I did ponder. I wondered what the boys truly felt. Would they miss me if I quit? Did I still have something I could offer them?

I continued to wonder about it all night and the next day as I prepared to go to the funeral. I wondered if the boys in the troop would be there. They were. All of them, except Sam. Marissa sent some flowers on Sam's behalf.

I had been to visit with Sam every day and was pleased with the progress he was making. He wouldn't look me in the eye, and I knew he was uncomfortable about what had happened. Marissa said it was because he felt guilty knowing he wasn't where he should have been that night—where he told her he would be. He seemed discouraged and depressed, but I reminded him of good times scouting, which seemed to lift his spirits considerably.

The doctor said that if he continued to progress, he would be out of the hospital within a week. The boys in the scout troop had planned a potato bar dinner and an auction to raise money to help with the hospital bills, and Marissa, always gracious and kind, expressed her gratitude. I just smiled and told her everyone wanted to help.

*****

I sat in the back for the funeral, knowing Mr. Handon didn't want me there. But I looked up and saw all my boys sitting on the two benches reserved for the pallbearers—Alex's troop and friends. I felt a great love for those boys, and I was grateful they had that honor. There were around twenty of them, with those who had moved away coming back and the younger ones that had joined our troop. Every one of them genuinely seemed like a son to me.

As I sat back there, feeling very alone, waiting for the funeral to start, someone sat by me and put an arm around my shoulders. I lifted my eyes to see who it was, and it was Rod. Behind his rough exterior, I could see the glimmer of tears in his eyes. Not trying to show much emotion, he gave me a quick pat and nodded as he dropped his arm, and I knew he understood.

I thought of the time the boys had tried to throw me in the lake and how he said he was there to back me up. He, indeed, had been there to back me up and still was. I appreciated it more than I ever had before.

The funeral was nice, at least as nice as funerals can be. David was one of the speakers and shared some of the scouting adventures he had been on with Alex, as well as some Alex had told him about. He talked of the time on the mountain when we had taken shelter from the thunderstorm and how I said I would always be the last man off the mountain. He said that after that, Alex always said that someday he would be a scoutmaster, and he, too, would be the last man off the mountain. I was sure David's relationship with his father had been strained over Alex's death. I could hardly hold back the tears as he said something else which I had thought about myself. David quietly spoke, as if deep in thought, and said, "I bet he would have been a great scoutmaster if he had lived to have had that opportunity."

By the time the funeral was over, my emotions were near the breaking point. I again sought the solitude of the scout room. As I sat, looking at the pictures on the wall, wondering if I could find it within myself to continue leading these boys, God once again intervened in his slow, but methodical, way in my life.

20
Heaven's Intervention

As I sat in the quiet of the scout room, I heard the doorknob's click, turned to see it open, and saw a small boy peer through. I tried to push my tears away and force a smile. "May I help you?"

The boy looked at the floor and spoke timidly. "I, uh, heard there was a scout troop here, and I saw the sign on the door, and well, I was wondering if anybody can join."

"Sure, any boy who is at least twelve can join."

"Really?!"

I smiled at his enthusiasm. "Really."

I looked at him. He was small, and I could hardly believe he was much past ten years of age, but I knew I was often wrong about the younger boys, so I thought I had better ask. "So, how old are you?"

"Twelve. I just turned twelve last week."

"What's your name?"

"Caleb," he answered. "Caleb Jacobson."

"Where do you live?"

He pointed toward the wall to the east. "In the house across the parking lot."

"Really?" I said, trying not to act too surprised.

No one had lived in that house for at least five years, and I knew it wasn't in any condition to live in.

"Really," he answered. "And where it was close, Mom said I could join the troop if there was one."

"Is your mother home right now?" I asked.

Caleb nodded.

I stood up, went to the filing cabinet, and pulled out an

enrollment form. "Then I would suggest that we go see if she will sign the enrollment form right now."

His face beamed with pleasure and excitement. As we walked across the parking lot, Caleb chattered away. By the time we reached his house, I already knew that his father had left them, and they had run out of money and food. They couldn't pay the house payments and lost their house, so they had moved here because the price of the house was low, and his mother had gotten a job at a local department store. After school each day, he had to babysit a younger brother and two little sisters.

As we stepped onto the doorstep, it groaned beneath my weight, and I wasn't sure it wouldn't give way. From up close, the house looked even worse than I had noticed from driving past it over the many years.

Caleb pulled the door open, invited me in, and then ran into the back, yelling. "Mom! Mom! There's a man here to see you."

I could hear a woman ask nervously, "Who is it?"

Caleb sounded proud and sure. "I think he's the scoutmaster."

The woman came into the living room and looked at me. "Yes, may I help you?"

I tried to smile reassuringly and reached out my hand. "My name is Tom Johnson. I'm the scoutmaster. Your son said he would like to be in our troop."

She nodded and shook my hand. "I'm glad to meet you. I'm Susan Jacobson." Then motioning to a chair, she said, "Won't you have a seat?"

As she sat down on the old couch, I dropped into an oversized chair that was across from it. I wasn't sure I would stop before I hit the floor. It had obviously seen better days, and when it finally did support my weight, I could feel a spring poking me in the backside. I adjusted, trying to get a more comfortable position, but no other position seemed any better.

Meanwhile, a little boy peeked into the room. I figured he was about eight, then reconsidered that if Caleb was twelve, as small as he was, the boy might be as old as ten. Then two little girls raced into the room and climbed onto the couch by their mother. I figured the oldest was somewhere between six and eight and the youngest was about four.

Susan smiled a weary smile at me. "I really would like to have Caleb have a chance to be in the scouts. I probably can't pay the dues until I get my first paycheck."

"Oh," I said, "there are no dues."

She looked surprised. "But I thought it would cost to be in scouts."

"Well, there are some costs associated with scouting, but we do a fundraising drive, and the entire community helps pay all the costs. We want every boy to have the experience, and we don't want anyone left out."

"Not even for a uniform or anything?"

"Not for anything. One of the ladies on our scout committee has a closet full of uniforms she maintains for the boys, and all the equipment and supplies are donated."

"Oh," is all she said, but her smile showed great relief.

I stood and handed her the enrollment form. "If you want to fill this out, on Tuesday when we have scouts, we'll see if we can have some uniforms there so we can fit him."

She asked Caleb to get her a pen from her purse, and he darted off and was soon back. He leaned over her as she filled it in, coaching her on the various parts. Finally, she pursed her lips and took a deep breath. "Caleb, I know how to fill out a form. I've been doing it since long before you were born."

Caleb took the slight scolding and pulled back, but he kept glancing over her shoulder, only to have her look at him to make him back off again. While she was filling it out, I looked around the house, and I suddenly had a wonderful idea of how we could help Caleb feel part of our troop.

When she finally handed it back, I thanked her and then approached the next subject carefully. "You know, Susan, I have a favor to ask."

She looked at me almost suspiciously. "Yes?"

"Your house hasn't been lived in for a long time, and my boys need some service hours for their rank advancements. Would you mind if we came over and helped fix things up a bit?"

"I . . uh, I can't afford to . . ."

"Oh, it would be at no cost. A big part of scouting is learning to serve. The men in the community would supply material and help. The boys could help on the lawn or anything else you wanted."

Her reluctance seemed to fade away. "That would be nice. I really was hoping to put in a garden."

"Great!" I replied. "I've got a rototiller, and we'll work up the soil and get it ready. We can also get you in a new lawn and all sorts of things."

Her smile widened further. "That would be nice."

"If you don't mind," I added, "I would like to send a few ladies from our church over to visit with you about your needs, and we will work it out with them and the men to organize it. If Caleb could come to scouts on Tuesday, he could work with our senior patrol leader to set things up, and we should be ready to work the Saturday after that."

"Okay. Thank you," she said.

"One last thing," I said. "Next Friday evening, we are having a baked potato bar dinner to raise money to help pay for some hospital bills for one of our scouts. I would like you and your family to be my guests at the dinner so you can meet my wife. I have some daughters about your daughters' ages, and I'm sure your children would enjoy it. You could also get to know lots of people from the community."

Susan nodded. "I would like that."

"Okay, scouts is Tuesday at seven o'clock, and we'll walk over to get you at about five forty-five next Friday for the dinner that starts at six o'clock. Dress is casual."

She smiled. "We'll be ready."

I was about to leave when she asked the kids to leave so she could talk to me alone. I couldn't think of anything else she would want to talk about, but I waited for her to speak after the children had gone.

After they had gone into the back and shut the door, she turned back to me. "I suppose Caleb told you about our situation?"

"He told me some."

"How much do you know?"

"I know that Caleb's father left, and you were not able to pay your bills and lost your home."

She nodded. "He actually left about a year ago, but he wasn't much of a father before that. That's why I hoped he could be in scouts, so he could have some men he could look up to."

"I'll do my best."

"Thank you," she said.

As I left, I thought about Sam and how Marissa had said something similar. The thought of being able to help the Jacobsons made me feel better. I have found that serving others always seems to take away discouragement.

I took Hannah over to meet Susan later that evening. She invited Susan to church, and Susan accepted. We arrived early enough on Sunday to walk over to the Jacobson home and walk back with them to church so they would feel comfortable. I introduced Caleb to the other boys, and they kindly took him into their group. They didn't comment on the fact that his clothes were old and worn or anything, but just made him one of them.

On Tuesday, Caleb was already at the church when I arrived for scouts. His enthusiasm rubbed off on the other boys and injected itself into our troop, which needed it desperately after the events of the last week.

As we planned the potato bar dinner and auction for Friday, and the service project for Saturday, the boys worked efficiently so they could still have some time for basketball. We had a good game, but I couldn't get myself into the spirit of it. The recent events still hung over me.

The week seemed to drag by, though I tried to keep busy to keep my mind off of the feelings I felt. When Friday came, all the boys met at five o'clock to help set up the tables for the dinner. All the boys had brought things for the auction. Some listed work hours like lawn mowing or other things to help raise money.

At five-thirty, the ladies started arriving with pans of baked potatoes wrapped in tin foil, bowls of cheese, onions, gravies, and many other toppings. Some had brought sheet cake for dessert. The men had organized making homemade root beer. I took Hannah and our children, along with Caleb, to walk over and get Caleb's family.

When we returned, I paid the suggested donation for both of our families. It was a wonderful evening. Marissa's family received a lot of money, almost ten thousand dollars. The only sad part was that everyone had hoped Sam would be there, but he ended up still being in the hospital. However, Marissa and the rest of her family came. She hugged and thanked everyone. And by the time the evening ended, I felt better. But I also thought that it would probably be good for the boys to have a new scoutmaster, someone with whom they could have a fresh start to leave these sorrowful events behind.

21

The Last Man Off the Mountain Again

Saturday was chilly but clear. I hurried and finished what chores I had at home so I could be at the church before eight o'clock. I loaded up my tiller and was soon on my way, arriving at the church fifteen minutes or so ahead of the scheduled time. Caleb must have been watching from his house because I had barely stepped from my pickup before he was standing beside me.

He chattered away happily. He seemed to relish, much more than the work we would do on his home, the thought of being with the boys again. I smiled at his exuberance.

The other boys trickled in, many bringing their fathers. At eight o'clock, we headed across the parking lot to Caleb's house. We didn't need to wait for everyone to gather since we knew they would see us working and come on over.

Caleb was proudly in charge. As soon as I had my tiller unloaded, he was there to show me where his mother wanted the garden. He helped show the other boys what needed to be done, and Rod and I organized them into different tasks.

The men organized into different groups as well. One, a plumber, was going through all the plumbing in the house, replacing anything that needed to be fixed. He had donated both his time and the material. Another was an electrician and was making sure the wiring was good.

Those with carpentry skills worked on the structure, especially the windows and doors, to ensure they were sound and sealed against the weather. The old house had stood vacant for so long that some of the doors and windows didn't close properly. These were taken off and realigned. Some of the men started scraping the house while others began the sticky job of painting with paint that had been donated.

I was glad to be working the tiller so I wouldn't have to paint. There are few household jobs I hate more than that one. The boys were another story. All of them begged for that job. But old Mr. Richins said that giving a boy scout a paintbrush and paint was second only to giving them a can of gasoline and matches for asking for problems. Thus, the boys were reluctantly shooed back to pulling weeds and removing rocks from the garden and lawn. The lawn would have to be tilled and replanted since it had died during the long years of neglect.

When I finished tilling the garden, I checked how the boys were coming on their assignments. I found Rod supervising the weed and rock removal on the lawn in front of the house. He and a group of boys were gathered around an especially large rock that had yet defied all their efforts to remove it.

Gordy, as usual, was sharing his knowledge on the subject. "I tell you that you are all a bunch of wimps. If you knew how to handle a shovel like I do, this job would be done by now."

Rod held out a shovel. "Why don't you show us, Gordy?"

Gordy put the shovel beside the rock and then, with both feet, jumped on it. The shovel hit a portion of the rock that was hidden under the ground, and the handle bounced back, smacking Gordy right in the nose, laying him out flat on his back on the ground.

As the group of boys roared with laughter, Rod, barely able to control his own mirth, reached out and helped Gordy to his feet. "I'm not sure I caught your technique, Gordy. Perhaps you better show us again."

The other boys burst out in laughter once more as Gordy growled sarcastically. "Ha, ha, ha. Very funny. Thousands of comedians out of work, and I get stuck with you."

I left them and went to find the others in the troop. As I was coming around the corner of the house, I stopped. Caleb was directing Jared and Tanner in clearing weeds from an old flower bed. But it was what they were saying that made me pause.

"I'd say you are lucky to have moved here," Jared said to Caleb.

"Why?" Caleb asked.

"Why?" Jared replied. "Because we have the best troop in the area, that's why."

"Heck," Tanner chimed in, "we got the best troop anywhere. And the best two scoutmasters, too."

"Our scoutmaster, Tom, makes the best fajitas in the world," Jared added.

"And don't forget the scones," Tanner added. "And if you aren't an expert outdoorsman, you will be by the time Tom and Rod get through with you. Our campouts are the best."

I silently stood there as the two boys continued to extol the greatness of our troop. They then talked about each member of the troop, their assignments, and some things about them. I listened for a while. Deep in thought, I was reminiscing with their stories when a rumbling sound and squealing from the hill behind the house broke me out of my thoughts.

I ran to where the sound was coming from, and flying down the steep gravel embankment where Devin and Dallin in a little red wagon, with Mort pushing them at full speed. The wagon started picking up speed and soon outpaced Mort's ability to keep up. He fell headlong into the gravel while Devin and Dallin, in the runaway red wagon, raced faster and faster toward the canal at the bottom of the hill.

I could envision every conceivable injury possible when they crashed, which they obviously were going to do. I dashed toward the spot they were heading for, reaching it just after they went over the embankment and splashed into the freezing water.

The panic that had seized my heart was replaced with relief as they popped out of the water, laughing. They drug the wagon out of the canal, and we were immediately surrounded by the other boys eager for a turn.

"Where did you get the wagon?" Jared wanted to know.

"It was in the old garden shed at the back of the property,"

Devin replied.

Rod looked at Gordy and said, "Hey Gordy, why don't you look in the shed and see if you can find some old handcuffs or an electric fence charger?"

"Ha, ha, ha," Gordy said. "Very funny. Thousands of comedians out of work, and I get stuck with you."

Everyone else laughed, and the other boys clamored for a chance in the wagon as Mort showed up, scraped and bleeding, from his tumble. He wasn't hurt badly, but I felt he needed some first aid. To the boys' disappointment, I confiscated the wagon and locked it in my pickup so there wouldn't be any further mishaps. I sent Devin and Dallin home to get dry clothes, and I retrieved the first-aid kit from the scout room to bandage Mort's cuts.

By the time I had him bandaged up and had returned to work, Devin and Dallin were back, and everyone was busy with their assigned tasks again. The morning continued to fly by, and before we knew it, the ladies of the community were arriving with sandwiches and lemonade for everyone. As we gathered for lunch, we had another surprise. A car pulled up, and there was Sam. When I saw the car, I thought it couldn't be. But when I looked closely, I could see it was indeed Sam.

The boys all rushed to the car, and Sam grinned as they jerked the door open and wanted to know how he was doing. Sam still looked thin and pale, but he seemed happier than I had seen him in a while.

Marissa came around from the driver's side and shooed the boys back enough that she could get the old wheelchair out of the back seat. She pulled it out and set it up. She didn't need to help Sam into it, however. All the boys clamored to do it. When Sam was finally situated, Marissa turned to me.

"Sam insisted on coming. He said if the troop was going to be working here today, he wanted to be here."

I couldn't talk, so I just nodded. She then reached into the car and pulled out a big plate of brownies. All the boys eyed them as she placed them on Sam's lap. She went behind Sam and pushed him right up to face me.

He lowered his head as he spoke. "We heard from the bishop that you felt someone else should be scoutmaster and you should be released because of what happened." All the other boys turned and looked at me in shock as Sam continued. "I know that Alex and I are the reason you don't feel you should be scoutmaster anymore. But I want you to know that what happened wasn't your fault, no matter what Alex's dad says."

He then held up the plate of brownies. "Mom made these for me to give to you in hopes you would change your mind."

I took the brownies, and the boys all crowded around.

"You aren't really thinking of not being our scoutmaster, are you, Tom?" Gordy asked.

I shrugged, embarrassed at the commotion and attention. "I just thought that maybe someone else could do a better job, and you guys could use a new start."

"No way!" Gordy said emphatically. "That's crazy talk."

All the other boys joined in, saying the same thing. Rod pushed through the circle and put his hand on my shoulder. "You know, if you quit, so do I. I only signed up to be your assistant."

I was at a loss as the boys all threw in their reasons I should stay. "You've got to stay," Mort said. "You've got to be there to make sure Gordy doesn't blow the rest of us up or something."

"Blow you up?" Gordy said. "It was your fireworks!"

"And you need to be there to make sure Mort and Gordy don't handcuff themselves to a grizzly bear or a moose or something," Devin added.

"Ha, ha," Gordy grunted. "Very funny. Thousands of comedians out of work, and I get stuck with you guys."

"Besides," Tanner added, "who will help me get my eagle?"

I chuckled slightly. "But Tanner, you never get your paperwork in."

"Maybe I will someday if you keep reminding me."

I looked around at the faces of these boys I had grown to love so much, their eager expressions saying even more than their words had.

"Well," I said. "I suppose if I can still do some good, then perhaps I can stay."

The boys let out a cheer. Gordy jumped behind Sam's wheelchair and grabbed the handles. "Race you all back to the sandwiches."

Rod seemed to sense that Marissa wanted to talk to me further, so he left to join the boys.

Marissa waited until they were all a distance away, then she turned to me. "When the bishop told us that you planned to leave the troop, Sam was heartbroken. It made me remember how I had almost kept him out of the troop because I was too overprotective. I'm glad I didn't."

I nodded. "I'm glad you didn't, too."

She looked right into my eyes as she continued. "I realize now that you would do anything for these boys and would do everything you could to protect and help them, and I had nothing to fear. In fact, as I told you before, you have become more of a father to Sam than his own father ever was."

She then smiled that smile where her mouth turned up at the corner, the same way Sam's did. As she did, her eyes filled with tears. "Thank you."

I couldn't speak, so I just nodded. As she climbed into her car and drove away, I turned to carry the plate of brownies over to share with the boys—my boys. I thought of each of them and the times we had shared together. I also thought of Caleb and how his mother said he needed scouting. It was then that I knew that, as long as those boys needed me, I would always be the last man off the mountain.

If you enjoyed this book, please a review on Amazon at:

Read stories, purchase books, find inspiring plays and musicals, get reseller discounts, or subscribe to our short story list by going to:
http://www.publishinginspiration.com

Daris Howard's Amazon page:
http://amzn.com/e/B004H76UGK